Untimely Death

Untimely Death

A Shakespeare in the Catskills Mystery

Elizabeth J. Duncan

CROOKED
LANE

NEW YORK

Published in the United States by Crooked Lane Books, an imprint of The Quick Brown Fox & Company LLC.

Crooked Lane Books and its logo are trademarks of The Quick Brown Fox & Company LLC.

Library of Congress Catalog-in-Publication data available upon request.

ISBN (paperback): 978-1-62953-826-6
ISBN (hardcover): 978-1-62953-191-5
ISBN (ePub): 978-1-62953-204-2
ISBN (Kindle): 978-1-62953-652-1
ISBN (ePDF): 978-1-62953-653-8

Cover design by Matthew Kalamidas/StoneHouse Creative
Cover illustration by Stephen Gardner.
Book design by Jennifer Canzone.

Printed in the United States.

www.crookedlanebooks.com

Crooked Lane Books
34 W. 27th St., 10th Floor
New York, NY 10001

Hardcover Edition: November 2015
Paperback Edition: November 2016

10 9 8 7 6 5 4 3 2 1

For Lucas and Riley

I fear too early, for my mind misgives
Some consequence yet hanging in the stars
Shall bitterly begin his fearful date
With this night's revels, and expire the term
Of a despisèd life closed in my breast
By some vile forfeit of untimely death.
But he that hath the steerage of my course,
Direct my sail. On, lusty gentlemen.

Romeo and Juliet, Act 1, Scene 4, Lines 107–114

Chapter 1

"Rupert! Car coming! Over here, you silly dog!"

A small dog with short legs and a happy grin bounded toward the woman holding a leather leash. "Good boy!" she said as she bent over, clipped the leash to his bright-red harness, and lovingly ruffled the fur behind his upright ears.

The woman, wearing a dark-green down jacket and wooly hat against a biting March wind, stood with her dog well back from the edge of the gravel driveway as a car driven by a middle-aged blonde woman swept past. Although the man in the passenger seat had his head turned away from her, Charlotte Fairfax recognized him as someone she'd hoped never to see again. *Keep going; don't stop*, she thought.

When the car had passed, Charlotte breathed a sigh of relief, and she and her dog continued walking up the drive toward Jacobs Grand Hotel.

Although the grandness had disappeared a decade or two ago, some faded dignity remained. The white-stuccoed main house, with its windowed gables and a large room on either side of the entrance portico, had welcomed guests in search of rest and relaxation since 1956. In the early days, couples and individuals stayed in the hotel proper, and families were booked into the bungalows that dotted the grounds. Everyone gathered in the hotel dining room for meals; entertainment was provided day and night in various function rooms. Once bursting with warm hospitality, a sense of community, and a never-ending list of indoor and outdoor activities, the hotel was now quiet and still as it shook off the last of winter and waited for summer to come around once again.

Jacobs Grand Hotel isn't hard to find. Drive along a gently curving blacktop road about one hundred miles north-northwest of New York City, and as the woods start closing in and the majestic Catskill Mountains emerge out of the mist, you come to a series of picturesque towns and villages. One of these is Walkers Ridge, a postcard-perfect community of about three thousand souls, proud of their hometown with its charming village green and white clapboard church, adorned by the finest pointed steeple outside New England.

It was here, on rural land a little ways out of town, that Esther and Joseph Jacobs chose to build their hotel.

Jacobs Grand Hotel flourished until the late 1970s, when a younger demographic with easy access to affordable international flights and a desire for globe-trotting independence sent it and many other all-inclusive, family-owned resorts in the Catskills into decline.

Many hotels mysteriously burned to the ground. Other properties in this land that time almost forgot were simply abandoned and reclaimed by nature, becoming eerie, overgrown reminders of long-ago afternoons filled with the excited shouts of children at tennis matches and pool parties. But the Jacobs family was one of a handful that managed to keep their business afloat.

Harvey Jacobs, grandson of Esther and Joseph and current owner of the hotel, credited his late mother with saving it. It had been her idea to hold a Shakespeare festival one summer; a large ground-floor function room near the kitchen had been converted into a small theater with a proscenium stage. Nearby storage rooms had been turned into dressing rooms, and somehow, it had all worked out.

As the festival established itself, it became the one important attraction that distinguished Jacobs Grand Hotel from all the others, and year after year, the guests kept coming, filling up the hotel bedrooms. Shakespeare, it seemed, was always in style.

There had been many lean years when it seemed doubtful they'd be able to carry on. But now, the Catskills, and Walkers Ridge in particular, were teetering on the brink of a revival, and Harvey Jacobs, third-generation hotelier, was convinced that if they could just make it through this season—summer theater here at the hotel and then autumn performances in Albany—they would turn the corner. They'd survived the recession of the late 1980s and the bank scandals of the new century, and they were almost home and dry.

He wasn't as involved in the theater operation as his parents and grandmother had been. In fact, while the hotel technically owned the theater company, he usually left the day-to-day running of it to theater people.

The longest-serving theater employee was Charlotte Fairfax, a slim, attractive woman in her early forties with shoulder-length brown hair, bright hazel eyes, and high cheekbones, who'd joined the Catskills Shakespeare Theater Company as head of the one-woman costume department about ten years ago.

As an up-and-coming costume designer with the Royal Shakespeare Company of Stratford-upon-Avon, she'd come to New York City for several months when the RSC was in town performing a play based on a Charles Dickens novel. Because the play featured so many actors, each playing several characters and thereby necessitating many costume changes, several wardrobe people were required to work as dressers to ensure that the production went smoothly.

She loved her job and considered herself fortunate to have been chosen for the Broadway assignment. But when her romance with one of the company's leading actors fell apart in the messiest way imaginable, she decided to remain behind in New York City when the company returned to Britain. Her career and her life had bottomed out, but she'd fought back and was grateful to Harvey Jacobs for giving her the chance to reestablish herself.

She wondered every now and then if she should have been more ambitious and worked on big Broadway productions like *The Lion King* or *Cats*, but she felt that her life was in a good place, and most of the time, she was content. The quiet life suited her. And besides, she'd grown up in an English village and knew that despite the outward appearance of dull tranquility, village life often hid long-held secrets and hearts of darkness.

Harvey Jacobs liked and trusted her. A few days ago, he'd told her that his nephew, Aaron, was taking a bit of time off from school and that starting next week, he would be working part-time in her costume department and part-time as the stage manager under the supervision of the theater's new director, Simon Dyer.

Charlotte and her beloved Rupert continued on their walk as the late afternoon sun washed the hotel in a gentle spring light. She loved the anticipation of this time of year, when the new cast members, most of them fresh from theater schools, arrived bursting with excitement for the season ahead, keen to start rehearsals, and all working toward the same goal of having the best opening night imaginable.

But this year was going to be different; changes were coming. She could just feel it.

Chapter 2

Death was no stranger to Charlotte. In fact, you could say she'd played a role—many times over—in twelve suicides, seven murders, and nine deaths in combat. For her, it was all in a day's work, because it was her job to make sure villains were dressed to kill and their victims were wearing clothes to die for.

And although she'd never been part of a real-life murder, that was about to change.

Charlotte had mixed feelings about having a part-time intern dumped on her this season. At the very least, she would have liked a say in the matter, but she was willing to keep an open mind and let him show her what he could do. If he was good, she'd be glad for the extra help. But if he wasn't, she had better things to do than find busywork to keep a New York City boy out of trouble.

"All right, Aaron, hang your jacket here, and then we'll go over the worksheet for today."

Charlotte crossed her arms and waited while the young man did as he was told.

Smiling, he sauntered over and stood beside her. "Okay," he said easily, folding his arms to mirror her stance. "Where would you like me to start?" In his early twenties, with dark curly hair and friendly brown eyes, he wasn't handsome in a traditional sense, but he was good-looking in a pleasant, contemporary way, like the actor who plays the wisecracking best friend in a romantic comedy.

"Before we get started, let's be clear about one thing. When you're told to be here at nine a.m., that means nine a.m., or even better, eight fifty-five so you can get your coat off and be ready to go on time. Understood?"

"Understood. My bad. Won't happen again." A sparkling smile underscored his sincerity.

"Good. Now the second thing you need to remember is this: costume is character. So everything we do here is critical to the success of the play. Most actors will tell you that their character isn't complete until they're in costume. And do you know what part of the costume really pulls everything together?"

"Their underwear?"

"The shoes. Know who told me that?"

Aaron shook his head.

"Sir Alec Guinness."

"Who?"

Charlotte groaned. "Never mind. Let's get to work. First, I'd best show you around. Follow me."

She led him past the costume department's worktable and a wall of shelves filled with end-of-bolt and remnant fabrics she'd bought deeply discounted or persuaded suppliers to donate to the theater company.

"Costume stock lives in here," Charlotte said as they entered an adjacent room. Rows of clothes protected by plastic dry-cleaner bags hung from portable rails. Every hanger had a yellow tag tied to it. Aaron lifted one and read it out loud.

"*Merchant of Venice*. Antonio, act one." He moved to the next tag. "*Merchant of Venice*. Bassanio, act one."

"There are lots of ways to organize these garments. You can group by men's and women's and then break those groups down by age group, but I've found the easiest way to store them is like this, by play and act. If there's a costume change within a scene, which happens rarely, you'll see two costumes for the character, labeled appropriately. The costumes are alphabetical, by play and character, so if you pull one, mind you put it back in the same place. With my system, I can find any garment I need quickly."

She placed her hand on the shoulder of a costume and adjusted its place ever so slightly on the rack.

"Our budget is small so we have to adapt existing costumes." She shrugged. "Let out the waist, add a bit of trim here or a ruffle there. Whatever. We're all about 'make do and mend' here. We can't design and create new costumes from scratch for each production, unfortunately. Coming as you do from fashion-design school, I hope that won't be too much of a disappointment." She waved a hand down a row of costumes. "You can take a closer look at these later."

"Your accent," Aaron said. "You're British, aren't you?"

"I am. English. Norfolk born and bred. I've lived in America for a long time, but never quite managed to lose the accent."

"Well, I like it. It suits you."

"I'm glad you think so, because it's the only one I've got."

They returned to the main workroom, and Charlotte pointed out an elderly black sewing machine in the corner, next to a smaller worktable. "This is handy for keeping pattern pieces on," Charlotte said, touching the table with her fingertips. "Because we're such a small company, we have to do everything ourselves, including the sewing, but that could be a very good thing for you. It's always best to know every aspect of a business, and while you're taking a bit of time off school, working here will keep your skills sharp." As she bent over the machine to show him how to wind a bobbin, loud voices from the hall caught their attention.

"Don't you think for one minute you've heard the last of this!" shouted a female voice to the sound of a slamming door. Charlotte and Aaron had just enough time to exchange puzzled looks before Lauren Richmond flounced into the room.

"What an idiot!" she exclaimed. Then, taking in Aaron, she said, "Oh! Who are you?"

"This is Aaron Jacobs," said Charlotte. "Harvey's nephew."

Lauren leveled her arrogant brown eyes at him until he looked away.

"Lauren's coming in at eleven for her first costume fitting," Charlotte said to Aaron. "She's playing Juliet. So I'd like you to—"

"Well, the thing is," interrupted Lauren, "I wonder if we could do it now. I'm meeting someone at eleven, so it would be better for me if we could just get this over with." She looked around the room, setting an open energy drink can on the worktable. Charlotte frowned at it but said nothing.

"Very good. Let's get started." Charlotte tipped her head in the direction of the room where the costumes were stored, and understanding her unspoken instruction, Aaron trotted off. Charlotte turned to her desk and picked up a small metal box. She opened it, flipped through the contents, and pulled out a card. She set it down on the desk and folded her arms, waiting for Aaron to return with the costumes.

A few minutes later, he appeared, arms outstretched and covered with light, flimsy dresses. "I found five," he said.

"That'll be about right," said Charlotte. "We won't get to all of them today, and we'll compare the costumes against my copy of the script later. Let's see what you've got."

She picked up the first garment and checked the tag: "*Romeo and Juliet.* Juliet, Act 1, Scene 3."

"Hmm. Yes. This is her entrance, if I recall. As good a place to start as any." She handed the dress to Lauren. "If you wouldn't mind, please go behind the screen and slip into this. And then come back to us, and we'll soon have you sorted and on your way." She looked at Lauren's feet. "And I'd like you to take off those high heels, so we can get an accurate idea of the length."

She checked the accessories card she had just pulled from the box. "It comes with a little hat and a large silver cross," she said to Aaron. "And ballet flats. Beige." She looked at Lauren. "You'll be wearing ballet flats. We'll get you a pair."

"I don't like wearing shoes that someone else has worn. I'll bring my own."

"Fine, but you don't have them here now, do you? And I'll want to approve them to make sure they look period appropriate. So for today, we'll do this in your bare feet."

"I'm not going to walk around this floor in my bare feet. It's probably filthy."

"Keep your shoes on until you come back to us in the costume, then." She turned to Aaron. "Look in that cupboard over there and you'll see a roll of pattern paper. Cut off a strip about two feet wide and bring it over here. Use the paper scissors, not the fabric scissors." She held up a pair with black handles. "These ones. Lauren can stand on the paper whilst we fit her. Cut off just enough for her to stand on. We don't waste anything around here, remember." Lauren disappeared behind the screen with the dress, and Charlotte waited.

Aaron returned with a piece of brown paper and set it on the floor where Charlotte pointed. And then they both waited. Aaron leaned against the back of the worktable, a large solid block with built-in drawers and a flat surface for making and cutting patterns. An old-fashioned yard-stick for measuring fabric was screwed down on one side, and two metal rulers, one L-shaped and the other a hip curve, were neatly arranged in one corner.

With a questioning glance at Charlotte and a slightly dismissive shrug of his shoulders, Aaron wandered off to explore the fabric selection. He ran his fingers along the bolts, examining the rich burgundy of the damasks and deep green of the brocades, heavy woolens, velvets, tartans, and flannels. On the lighter side, silks, satins, and taffetas in pale colors of pink, cream, and blue would be used as linings and to provide contrast through the slashing of sleeves.

"The fabric choice indicates the class or social status of the character," Charlotte remarked. Pleased that he was showing an interest in the material, she was about to elaborate when Lauren emerged from behind the screen and walked to the piece of brown paper laid out for her.

Even in a seventeenth-century costume paired with twenty-first-century high heels, she looked stunning. *Oh, this one is going to be a pleasure to dress, but a challenge, too*, Charlotte thought. Tall and perfectly proportioned, her dark hair falling in loose curls around her face, she looked the part of Juliet, even if she was a decade or so older than the achingly young Juliet of the play.

"How does the dress feel?" asked Charlotte.

"It's a little tight across the back and in the chest," Lauren replied, wriggling her shoulders. The costume consisted of a cream-colored sleeveless underdress with a gold embroidered waistband and a dusty pink overdress, open at the front.

"Take your shoes off," said Charlotte. Lauren did as she was told, and Charlotte removed the tape measure that always hung around her neck and adjusted her dark-framed glasses. "Stand up straight, please." She measured Lauren's bust, hips, and back from the nape of her neck to her waist. "We'll have to adjust the darts for allowance," she said to Aaron. "If we can't get that right, you can make a new top for it."

"A new top?" said Lauren. "You must be joking! I would expect you to make me a new costume, not just put a new top on a shabby old skirt." She pinched the overdress at the sides and lifted them up.

"I was just explaining to Aaron that it's 'make do and mend' around here," said Charlotte in a level, measured tone. "We do the best with what we've got. Our resources are very limited."

"And why would he make my costume, anyway?" Lauren demanded. "Surely you would do that? You're the costume designer, aren't you? He's just your assistant! What does he know?"

"Quite a lot, actually. He's been to Parson's. He probably knows as much about fashion design as anyone."

"Do you know who I am?" demanded Lauren. "I'm going to be a huge star, and you're going to be very sorry you talked to me like that."

"Lauren, when you're a huge star, you can refuse to wear any costume you like. However, since huge stars like Judi Dench and Helen Mirren were happy with the stage-worn costumes I fitted for them at the Royal Shakespeare Company, I dare say these costumes will be just fine for you."

Charlotte paused for a moment to let those names sink in and gave Lauren a practiced, professional smile. "Right, then. Ready for the next one?"

"I don't feel like doing any more today," said Lauren, her lips drawn down in an unbecoming, whiney pout. "You have my measurements. I can come back later. I've had enough of this, and I don't want to be late for my eleven o'clock meeting."

She put her shoes on and flounced back behind the screen. Aaron opened his mouth to say something, but Charlotte gave her head a little shake and held up a warning finger. "Aaron," she said, "why don't you trot along to the canteen and bring us back some tea." She picked up a small piece of paper from her desk, wrote down a number, and handed it to him. "That's the account number for our department. Give it to the cashier. And if you don't like tea, get a coffee or whatever you want to drink." He turned the piece of paper over and examined the print on the back. He raised an eyebrow.

"I make scratch paper from the messages that come in overnight on the fax machine in the office," Charlotte explained. "I cut the page in four. With the paper scissors, not the fabric scissors." She touched a pair of silver shears on the worktable. "Those ones are to be used only for cloth. Nothing else. Silver handles for cloth only. Black handles for paper only. Right. Off you go, and while you're gone, I'm going to have a word with madam here." She tipped her head in the direction of the change screen. "You can take your time coming back."

Lauren tossed the dress over the screen and emerged from behind it in her street clothes.

"Yes, that's perfectly all right, Lauren," said Charlotte, with the tiniest hint of sarcasm. "Just leave the dress there, and we'll take care of it."

Lauren strode past her and had almost reached the door when the sound of Charlotte's voice stopped her.

"Lauren, before you go, I'd like a word, please."

Lauren turned. "Well? What is it? I'm in a hurry."

"Aaron's going to be here for the summer, working with all of us, and I'd like you to show him a bit of respect. His uncle is the owner of this hotel—and technically your employer—so you'd do well to keep that in mind. If you want to keep your job, that is."

Lauren laughed. "Oh, I don't think you need to worry about that. I'd say my job here is pretty secure."

Her footsteps faded down the hall, and as she disappeared around a corner, Aaron appeared from the other direction, balancing a small tray. "They said this is how you like your tea," he said to Charlotte as he entered the workroom.

She preferred her tea in a proper cup and saucer, but the best the canteen could do was a mug. Still, that was better than those awful disposable cups. The cup rattled a little against the tray as Aaron set it on Charlotte's desk.

Charlotte sighed.

"What's the matter?" asked Aaron as he picked up his paper coffee cup.

"We're going to have a problem with some of the women's costumes. They don't fit the younger women anymore."

Aaron raised an eyebrow as he took a sip of coffee.

"They get breast enlargements. Lauren's had hers done. The costumes are too tight across the chest. Why don't you have a good look at them?"

Aaron gave her an amused look, and Charlotte laughed.

"Her costumes, not her breasts. See if you can insert a gusset, saving us having to make all new tops. Think about it, make a few sketches, and we'll talk about it later."

Aaron cleared his throat and rubbed his hands together.

"Are you all right? What's the matter?" Charlotte asked.

"She was the last person I expected to see here. I don't know how Uncle Harvey could have hired her."

Chapter 3

When the hotel opened in the 1950s, what was now the theater had been a noisy bingo hall by day and a supper club by night, where up-and-coming comedians, dancers, crooners, and magicians had entertained ladies in strapless satin dresses and gentlemen in suits as they drank champagne and smoked cigarettes. Today, it was in use as a rehearsal room as Simon Dyer got the new season under way.

"All right, everybody. Quiet please. Places."

Simon walked onto the stage. In his early fifties, tall and trim with curly grey hair, he looked the part of a central casting theater director. It wasn't so much the beige trousers, blue shirt, and boating shoes. It was the yellow sweater draped over his shoulders and tied around his neck, not to mention the glasses on top of his head. But the real giveaway was the script in his left hand.

"All right," he repeated, raising his right hand to get the actors' attention. "This morning we're starting our *Romeo and Juliet* rehearsal at the beginning. Act one, scene one. And I don't want you to just go through the motions—I want to see some real acting here. Pay attention to the words. Listen to the way they sound. Think about what they mean. Put your heart into it. This is where you start to become your character."

He stepped off the stage, took a seat in the front row, threw one leg over the other, and stretched his arm along the back of the chair beside him. The actors, dressed in jeans and casual sweatshirts, exchanged words with one another as they took their places.

"We'll skip the prologue and start with the entrance of Sampson and Gregory. Right. Transport me to old Verona. Off you go." Simon eased himself back in his chair as the action began.

The young men playing the friends of Romeo swaggered their way around the stage, speaking their lines of easy, risqué banter for a few minutes to prepare the way for the entrance of Brian Prentice, who was appearing in this play in the relatively minor role of Romeo's father, Lord Montague.

Every year, the Catskills Shakespeare Theater Company managed to bring in a second-rate, almost but not quite down-on-his-luck British actor that most American theatergoers had never heard of. The accent was right, and it was hoped that the casting of an actor "direct from

London's West End" would boost sales and add a certain cachet of English authenticity to the productions. And this year, Brian Prentice was that actor.

The acting world is a small one, and Simon Dyer was well aware of Prentice's reputation, both good and bad. Great things had been predicted for him in the early stages of his career, although he hadn't been expected to come into his own until he'd matured into the meaty, king-sized Shakespearean roles. Now that he had reached the right age, his reputation for drinking threatened to eclipse everything he'd worked so hard for. Producers and directors weren't as tolerant of heavy drinking as they had been a generation or two earlier.

Simon had given him fair warning a couple of nights ago, and he hoped Prentice had taken his words to heart. He leaned forward slightly in anticipation of Prentice's entrance.

On cue, Prentice entered stage left, leaning just a little too heavily on the arm of the actress playing Lady Montague. And then he spoke.

"Thou villain, Capulet. Hold me, let me go."

Simon groaned inwardly. *Oh, God. Here we go. He can't even get his entrance line right.* He'd left out the word "not." He was meant to say, "Hold me not, let me go."

Simon rose slightly, ready to stop the action, but decided to let it play out for a few more minutes and settled back. Prentice spoke another couple of lines and then gazed off into the wings while the actor playing the prince delivered a rather long speech almost word perfect. Simon was impressed. And then everyone except Prentice and two other actors exited the stage. It was Prentice's turn to speak next, but he missed his cue as he continued to look off into the wings, frowning.

"Brian." Simon brought his attention back to the stage.

"Sorry," muttered Prentice. Then, seeming to refocus, he carried on: "Many a morning hath he there been seen, with tears augmenting . . ." His voice trailed off. "Sorry," he repeated. "Not quite with it this morning." He looked down at Simon in his front-row seat. "Can we take a break? I need a break."

Simon looked at his watch. Just past eleven. "Of course." He stood up and addressed the actors on stage. "Can you ask the others to join you?" When the rest of the actors required for this rehearsal had shuffled back on stage, Simon told them they were taking a twenty-minute break and they should be back and ready to go again at eleven thirty sharp.

Wanting a quiet word with Prentice, Simon walked along the front of the stage, mounted the steps that led to the wings, and searched the backstage area. Prentice was nowhere to be seen.

Chapter 4

At eleven thirty, the actors drifted back onstage, ready to pick up where they'd left off. Some clutched water bottles; others held scripts. They took their places, and the rehearsal resumed until Romeo confessed to Benvolio that he was in love with Juliet. They wrapped up the scene, and then Simon called the lunch break. "Back at one," he shouted as the actors headed off stage. "We'll start scene three."

Although he desperately wanted to speak to Prentice, he decided to let the man enjoy his lunch. And that would buy Simon time to consider what he needed to say and the best way to say it.

He slipped out a side door of the hotel into the grounds and then walked down the long drive, once lined with wooden benches, that led from the hotel to the main road and the lake beyond.

The weather was pleasant but brisk enough that he was glad he'd worn his jacket. He crossed the road and made his way down an overgrown path to two weathered Adirondack chairs that overlooked the lake. Peeling, rust-colored paint on the arms of the chairs revealed bare spots of grey wood beginning to splinter.

Simon leaned over each chair and rocked it gently from side to side. Choosing the one that felt marginally sturdier, he sat in it and gazed across the lake. A light mist hovered over the surface of the water and wreathed the bare trees that surrounded it.

He wondered briefly, as he often did, how his life had got so crazy that he'd ended up here. But after all that had happened, he reckoned he was lucky to have a job at all. A job that came with room and board—board being a meal ticket to the canteen, and room being the small bungalow beside Charlotte Fairfax's slightly larger one. He'd have to set up another meeting with her soon to go over the costume requirements and make sure everything was ready in time for the dress rehearsals scheduled to start in about six weeks. But he'd been in the theater business long enough to recognize a well-organized professional when he saw one. He didn't anticipate any problems in the costume department.

Where he did see trouble brewing, however, was with Brian Prentice. The drinking was going to be a problem, and if Simon wasn't mistaken, Prentice already had something going on with Lauren Richmond. *Be very careful when you stir the pot of desire, Brian*, he thought. *Especially when your bitch of a wife is hovering nearby and the object of your desire is out for what she can get. You're headed for trouble there, old son.* Tears before bed, as his old English gran used to say.

He checked his watch and, groaning, stood up.

*

"All right, everybody. Hope you had a good lunch, and now let's get back to work. Scene three. Clear the stage and let's go."

Once again seated in the front row, Simon stretched his long legs in front of him and waited. Two women hurried on stage. When one stepped toward the edge of the stage to speak to Simon, he waved a dismissive hand and told them to start.

"Nurse, where's my daughter? Call her forth to me," said the actress playing Lady Capulet. Her lines were met by the nurse's response.

"Now, by my maidenhead, at twelve year old,
I bade her come. What, lamb! what, ladybird!
God forbid! Where's this girl? What, Juliet!"

She held a hand over her eyes as if blocking out the sun and rocked sideways slightly. But Lauren did not appear. After a moment, the actor nearest to the wings called out, "Your cue, Lauren darling!"

Simon stood up and approached the stage. "What's the matter? Where is she?"

"That's what we wanted to tell you," said the actress playing Lady Capulet. "She isn't backstage."

"Oh, for God's sake," said Simon. "Where the hell is she?"

Aaron Jacobs stuck his head around the curtain. "I'll go find her."

"No, you won't," said Simon. "Come out from behind that curtain and get down here so I can talk to you without shouting."

Aaron descended the steps that led from the side of the stage and planted himself in front of Simon.

"I need you to find Charlotte. Tell her Lauren hasn't shown up for rehearsal. Find out from the cast mates what room Lauren's in and ask Charlotte to check it. Maybe she's fallen asleep or got the rehearsal time wrong or something. Tell Charlotte to phone me if Lauren isn't in her room." He handed Aaron a card. "Here's the number. And after you've spoken to Charlotte, you'd better come right back here in case you're needed. If Lauren hasn't shown up by the time you return, we'll have to find someone to stand in for her. We've got to keep this rehearsal moving. Got all that?"

Aaron nodded.

"Right. Off you go."

The older actors, well used to the hurry up and wait aspect of theater and cinema work, milled around the stage, talking amongst themselves in low voices. A few of the younger ones pulled out their phones and thumbed through them.

About ten minutes later, slightly out of breath, Aaron returned.

"Charlotte's gone upstairs to look for her," he said to Simon.

*

It had been a long time since Charlotte had been up to the hotel's second floor, but nothing had changed in years; the painted floorboards still creaked under the faded and frayed beige carpet runner that ran the length of the hallway. She checked the room numbers on the wooden doors that should have been replaced years ago to bring the building up to code.

The metal numbers *1* and *5* nailed to the door told her she'd arrived at Lauren's room. She knocked and waited. When there was no answer, she knocked again and, after a brief pause, tried the doorknob. She was a little surprised when it turned in her hand, and with a little pressure and a small creak, she opened the door a few inches.

"Lauren, it's Charlotte Fairfax," she said in a voice just slightly louder than a normal speaking tone. "Are you there? May I come in?"

When there was no response, she opened the door wider and, repeating Lauren's name, entered the room. The curtains were drawn, and it took a moment for her eyes to adjust to the semidarkness. She made out a chest of drawers on her left and an unmade bed on her right. Lying on the bed, fully dressed but her dark hair tousled, was Lauren. Hand held out, Charlotte approached her.

"Lauren! Wake up! You're late for rehearsal," she said. "They're waiting for you."

When Lauren did not move, she took a step closer to the bed and bent over the still figure.

Trying to quell the rising sense of panic by telling herself to remain calm, Charlotte gave Lauren's shoulder a gentle shake and repeated her name, a little louder this time and with more urgency. She then touched her cheek with a slightly trembling hand and bent down, placing her face close to the girl's. Lauren's breathing was ragged and shallow, and her breath was giving off a strange, unpleasant odor. Charlotte gave the sleeping girl one last shake and, unable to rouse her, hurried from the unnaturally quiet room.

Chapter 5

Lady Deborah Prentice steered the midsize American rental car up the long driveway that led to the Jacobs Grand Hotel. She slowed down and, fighting her deeply ingrained instinct to pull over onto the left shoulder, steered the car to the right as flashing lights behind her signaled the approach of an ambulance. When it had passed, she picked up speed and continued the rest of the way to the hotel and then drove around to the back and parked. She opened the rear door of the vehicle, lifted out two plastic carrier bags from Fifth Avenue stores, and entered the hotel through the service entrance. The long, empty back corridor led in one direction to the kitchens and in the other to the theater space, with the lobby and registration desk beyond that. She turned in the direction of the theater.

Lady Deborah was just an inch or two short of six feet tall and finely made. She had that distinctive translucent skin so admired among the English aristocracy, and her carefully and expensively tinted blonde hair was swept back behind her ears and tied neatly with a small black velvet bow. Her eyes were a pale blue and her top lip was thin, with a full, pouty lower lip. She wore pearl earrings and a double-strand pearl necklace. Her Burberry raincoat was undone, revealing a tailored dark green suit. Her court shoes made no sound as she strode along the hallway, the Launer handbag she carried swinging gently in time with her steps.

A few minutes later, she pushed open a door marked "Backstage Area—No Admittance" and entered a large open space. A few plastic chairs were scattered around a concrete floor, but the area was empty. From somewhere off to her right came the muffled sound of voices. She turned toward them, pushed aside a couple of black curtains, and entered the wings. The actors were grouped together on the stage, some sitting on the floor, others standing.

"What's going on?" she asked in a cut-glass English accent. "An ambulance passed me in the drive. Is it Brian?"

"I'm all right, darling," Brian Prentice said, emerging from the shadows. "I'm fine. It's Lauren Richmond. She's poorly and been taken to hospital."

"Poorly? What on earth's the matter with her?"

"We don't know, Lady Deborah," Simon Dyer chimed in. "She didn't turn up on time for rehearsal, so I sent someone to look for her, and she was discovered unwell in her room. And now, as Brian just said, she's on her way to the hospital."

"If she's that unwell, I expect that's the best place for her," said Lady Deborah, in that clipped, British, no-nonsense way. "Well, I'll leave you to it, then." Brian took a step toward her as she turned to go.

"I'll come with you." He turned his gaze to Simon. "You're finished with me for the afternoon, I take it?"

Simon nodded. "If you're not feeling up to it, we'll just have to manage without you." He took a step closer and said in a lower voice so the other cast members couldn't hear him, "We need to talk again. And soon."

"If you're coming with me, Brian, then you can make yourself useful and carry these." Lady Deborah held out her carrier bags and, with an aggressive swipe, pulled the wings curtains aside, and the two left the stage, Brian trailing after her with a bag in each hand.

Simon watched Prentice and his wife leave and then opened his script and addressed the rest of the cast.

"Those of you not in the scene, clear the stage. The rest of you, places."

"What about me?" asked Aaron. "Do you need me anymore?"

"No," said Simon in a gentler tone. "Go back to what-ever it is you were doing."

*

Aaron opened the door to the costume department. The afternoon sun filtered through tall windows covered in a thin layer of winter dirt, casting long shadows and picking out the details of the worktable. Charlotte, her back to the door, was bent over her desk. She straightened at the sound of the door opening and turned slowly to see who it was.

"Oh, it's you. Good. Come in and tell me what's happening."

Aaron set a mug of tea on her desk. "Here. Thought you could use this."

She smiled at him. "Very thoughtful. Thank you. We didn't quite finish our office tour, but there's a little, well, you couldn't really call it a kitchen, but a cupboard with a sink and a kettle and a little fridge just through there." She pointed to a door off the main room. "It gets too expensive getting drinks in from the canteen, so I usually make my own tea. I just sent you to get drinks from the canteen this morning to give you something to do whilst I had a private word with Lauren. Normally we don't put our drinks on the account. That's just for special occasions."

"I didn't put these on the account, Charlotte. Paid for them myself."

"That was sweet of you. Thank you. But before you sit down, would you mind picking up that can Lauren left on the worktable and taking it into the kitchen? I can't believe I let it sit there all day. Too much going on, I suppose."

Aaron disappeared into the kitchenette with the can before returning and pulling up a chair beside Charlotte's desk.

"What are you working on?" he asked.

"Trying to sort out the rest of the costumes for all three plays in production this season. When I have the list complete, we'll have to check them. They're put away dry-cleaned and mended, so we should be all right. Then we have to set up fittings for every actor, every costume, every scene, every play. It's all very time consuming, so I'm glad you're here. Between us, we can do two actors at a time. But tell me. What happened at the rehearsal? How did the cast take the news about Lauren?"

"Well, nobody really said anything, but to be honest, I don't think anybody likes her very much. Then Lady What's-her-name showed up, and her and Brian left." He stifled a yawn.

"Aaron, you mustn't call her Lady What's-her-name. She's Lady Deborah. Her father's an earl. If you're going to make it in the fashion business, you've got to work on your professionalism. In the theater, actors expect to be treated with a certain amount of deference, and if you can't manage that, you should at least get people's names right. And it's not 'her and Brian left,' it's 'she and Brian left.' You wouldn't say, 'Her left,' would you?"

She sighed, took a sip of tea, and set the mug back down on the tray. Although she was only in her early forties, she suddenly felt old. She could hear her mother, a real stickler for good grammar, reflected in her own voice. "If you're going to make something of yourself, Charlotte," she'd said at least a thousand times, "you'll have to speak properly." But that was in Britain, where grammar and accents used to matter more than they did here in America.

"Sorry, Aaron," she said. "Starting to sound like my mother. In the end, we all turn into our parents."

"No worries."

"What did you make of Lady Deborah?"

"She seemed a bit stuck up. Like she thinks she's better than the rest of us."

"In England, we call that 'posh.'"

"Posh. Hmm. I like that word. Anyway, expensively put together, I'd say. Dressed way more formally than most people around here. Looked like she'd been shopping in the city. Had a couple of shopping bags from Saks and Barneys."

"Saks and Barneys, eh?" Charlotte pursed her lips and nodded slightly. "Right, well, let's get your work organized for the rest of the day. We've got to set up a meeting with Simon to offer our suggestions for costumes and to hear what he has to say. He may have some specific requests or ideas. The best directors always do. For example, he may need something done a certain way so it'll work with what the lighting designer has in mind."

Aaron made a little noise that seemed to indicate agreement. "That's interesting. Hadn't really thought of that. So when I'm designing for the runway, I need to keep lighting in mind."

"Oh, I can teach you all kinds of tricks that'll come in handy for the runway," Charlotte replied. "For example, say a script requires a character to pull a revolver out of his pocket and shoot somebody. What are the implications of that for us in costume design?"

Aaron thought a moment, and then his face brightened. "He has to be wearing a costume that has a pocket?"

"That's right! And not only must there be a pocket, it has to be deep enough and strong enough to hold the revolver." Charlotte paused, and then continued.

"Okay. So, this season we're opening with *Romeo and Juliet*, but we're also doing *King Lear* and *A Midsummer Night's Dream*. Here's the cast list for each play." She handed him a binder. "You'll see who's been cast in what part. Here's the big question. Have you read the plays?"

He shook his head. "Sorry, no."

She pointed to the bookshelf beside her desk. "You'll find all the Shakespearean plays there. The complete works. Help yourself. You'll have to be familiar with all three plays being performed this season, so if I were you,

I'd start this afternoon with *Romeo and Juliet*, as that's the first one up."

Aaron flipped a few pages in the binder. "This information would be so much better set up on a spreadsheet. That way, you could see who's playing what part in each play. And then, with one keystroke, you could sort the data by actors' names so you could look up Brian Prentice, say, and see immediately all the roles he's playing. So in effect, you'd know by play and by actor every costume that's required.

"You could replace your little card system with spreadsheets of all the details on each actor. Measurements, roles, dates, and so on. You could print it out if you prefer working from paper and also have a record on your computer."

Charlotte looked at him in admiration. "That would be wonderful! Would it be a big job?"

Aaron shook his head. "Nope. I could start setting it up for you this afternoon. That, and reading *Romeo and Juliet*, of course."

Charlotte gave him a thumbs-up and then pulled a slightly tattered paperback copy of *Romeo and Juliet* from the bookshelf and slid it across the desk to him.

"This Brian Prentice guy," said Aaron thoughtfully, as he picked up the book and glanced at the cover.

"Yes. What about him?"

"Well, it's just that when his wife arrived . . ." he looked up from the book and continued, "Lady Deborah . . .

when she arrived, the first thing she said was something like, 'Is it Brian? Is he okay?'"

"So?"

"That just seemed a bit weird. Why would she think something had happened to Brian? I mean, if I saw an ambulance in the drive, I wouldn't automatically assume it was there for a specific person. Why did she think the ambulance was there for Brian?"

"Well, it's pretty well known that Brian's got a drinking problem, so she might have thought something had happened to him. He's been drinking heavily for a long time. That may be part of the reason he didn't do as well as people thought he would. His career never really took off the way it should have. At one time, he was a rising star, and the theater world expected great things from him. The next Laurence Olivier, everyone said. But he didn't live up to his promise, unfortunately."

"I guess that explains what he's doing in a place like this, then. I wondered about that." Aaron narrowed his eyes slightly and gave her a quizzical look. "His wife must have money of her own, because he's not buying stuff for her at stores like Saks and Barneys on what my uncle pays him."

"Speaking of your uncle, I think you should go and see him and make sure he's informed about what happened to Lauren."

*

Brian Prentice poured himself a couple of fingers of scotch, held the glass up to the light in a mildly pretentious gesture, tipped it slightly in his wife's direction, and then drained it.

Lady Deborah crossed her legs and gave him a level, measured look, tinged with the contempt she no longer took any pains to conceal.

"I had lunch in town with Harriette Ainsworth," she said. "She mentioned a reception at the British consulate coming up in a couple of weeks. They're invited. I wonder why we're not."

"Probably because the people at the consulate don't know we're here," Brian replied. "Why don't you ring them and let them know? Ask them to put us on the guest list. Or better yet, suggest they hold a reception for me."

"For you? I think they'd be more likely to hold one for me. Anyway, asking people to give a party for you doesn't seem like good form."

"Really, Deborah, nobody takes any notice of that sort of thing nowadays. If those consulate people had known we were here, they'd surely have invited us. Make the call, why don't you? You can be very persuasive. They'll put us on the standing guest list, and that'll give us six months of lovely parties with free drinks. Speaking of which . . ." He turned back to the drinks table and reached for the bottle.

"I think you've had enough, don't you?" Lady Deborah said in a voice dripping with ice. With a frustrated sigh, Brian set the bottle down and dropped heavily into the armchair at right angles to the sofa.

While the rest of the cast was housed in the former staff bedrooms on the second floor of the hotel, with room and board costs deducted from their wages, six months' accommodation in the bungalow reserved for the exclusive use of the season's star performer was included in Brian's contract. The two-bedroom dwelling was clean and comfortable but in sad need of a refurbishment. Brian's eyes wandered over the flowered curtains, worn brown carpet, and old-fashioned furniture. The back of his chair even had an antimacassar, and it was against this that his head now rested.

"God, I hate this place already, and we've only been here five minutes," he said, gazing up at the water-stained ceiling.

"Oddly enough, I rather like it," said Deborah. "Reminds me a little of nanny's old flat when I was a girl. Which we only got to see if we'd been very good. It was always such a treat to have our tea there. Of course, her flat wasn't nearly as shabby as this place—Mummy saw to that—but still."

Brian shifted in his chair. "I think I'll have a bit of a lie down before dinner."

"You do that. It's getting a bit late now, but I'll ring the consulate on some pretext or other tomorrow and try to wrangle an invitation to the party. I don't suppose you've lost your passport, have you?"

"No, I haven't. Why do you ask?"

"It's just that a lost passport would be the perfect excuse to ring them. Oh well. I'll think of something. As you say, I can be very persuasive."

As he stood up, she gave him a sly look and remarked, "You know, a party at the consulate would be just the thing. Give us the chance to mix with a better class of person. Not to mention a perfect opportunity to give a ring or brooch a bit of an airing. People do so enjoy seeing a little something from the splendid Roxborough collection every now and then."

Brian hesitated for a moment in the doorway and then disappeared into the bedroom, chased by the sound of her shallow laughter.

Chapter 6

A very tired Harvey Jacobs took off his rimless glasses and rubbed his eyes as his nephew entered his office. A robust man in his early fifties with a rather large waist, Harvey wore the same style of striped trousers as his father had, made by the same tailor. A pair of hardworking suspenders struggled to hold the trousers in place over his bulging stomach. His blue striped shirt had large wet patches under the arms, although his office was not particularly warm. He'd been told more than once that he bore an uncanny resemblance to Theodore Roosevelt. Harvey would laugh it off, but secretly he took it as a compliment.

A glass-fronted bookshelf filled with green ledgers, leather guest books, and black cloth binders covered one wall. Bankers boxes, some with lids askew, were piled against another wall. A silver desk set featuring a cut-glass inkwell and penholder on an inscribed silver tray was almost lost in the clutter on the heavy oak desk. A green metal "in" tray on a wire stand was overflowing, while the "out" tray beneath it was empty.

Harvey gestured at the visitor's chair.

"How are you, Aaron? Enjoying your first day on the job?"

"Don't know if 'enjoy' is the right word, but yeah, it's going okay. Not what I expected, though, and very busy."

"Keeping you busy, are they? Good. What have you been doing?"

"Working with Charlotte in costumes, mostly. I offered to set up an Excel spreadsheet for her so she could track actors in their plays more easily." Aaron cast an eye around his uncle's office, thinking it would take more than a spreadsheet to clean up this mess. *There must be decades of papers here, all in apparently no order.* And the tax situation! If the IRS came calling . . . He shuddered.

"And don't forget you've got the stage manager job to do, too," his uncle said. "I guess Charlotte and Simon will have to work out a schedule for you. Or you can go where you're needed, as and when. Up to them to make it work."

"Yeah, okay. Listen, I can see you're busy, so I won't take too long. Charlotte asked me to make sure you know what happened today. With Lauren."

"Who?"

"Lauren Richmond. This season's ingenue."

"Oh, right. What about her?"

"She didn't show up for rehearsal on time, so Simon had Charlotte check on her, and she found her in her room, sick, so an ambulance was called and now she's in the hospital."

"Good Lord! Why am I just hearing about this now? Is she all right? What's the matter with her?"

Aaron shrugged. "I don't know."

"Did someone from the theater company go with her to the hospital?"

"I don't think so."

"Right, well, I'll call the hospital and see if they'll tell me how she's doing."

As he reached across his desk, a towering pile of documents toppled over, spewing file folders, booklets, newspaper cuttings, and invoices over the floor.

"Don't worry about that. I know this looks like an awful mess, but I can put my finger on everything I need, when I need it. Just give me a moment and I'll find her contract details."

"Honestly, Harvey, I don't see how you could have hired her."

"Me? I didn't hire her. What do I know about acting? Simon casts the actors he wants." He gave his nephew a hard look. "Why? What's the matter with her? Is she no good? A bimbo?"

"This isn't about her acting ability. It's about who she is."

Jacobs frowned. "She's Lauren Somebody-or-other. Can't remember her last name."

Aaron stood up. "You don't get it, do you?"

"Look, Aaron. I don't know what the hell you're talking about, and frankly, I don't have time for this right now. I've got to make some phone calls." He picked up the telephone receiver and, realizing he didn't have a number, set it back in its cradle with a defeated sigh. "I wish Nancy were still with me. It was a sad day when we had to let her go. She was always so resourceful—she'd have known how to handle a situation like this. Probably would have gone to the hospital with the girl, phoned the parents, done all the right things."

He appealed to his nephew. "Can you find me the number of the hospital?"

Aaron sat down again, tapped his phone, and then looked around for a something to write on. Seeing nothing, he held up the screen to his uncle.

"I don't have my glasses on. Read it to me."

Jacobs picked up a pencil with fingers that looked like sausages that had been thawed too quickly and scribbled the number on the back of a document that had fallen out of a file folder when the pile toppled over. And then, leaving his nephew to see himself out past the empty area where the highly efficient Nancy used to sit, and breathing a little heavily, Jacobs repeated the numbers under his breath as he punched them into his telephone.

*

Aaron entered the wardrobe room just as Charlotte picked up her ringing desk telephone. She listened for a few moments, made a few noises indicating agreement, and then said good-bye and put the phone down. Aaron raised an eyebrow.

"That was your uncle. He just spoke to the hospital. They did release some information on Lauren's condition to him, as she has no next of kin available, and as her employer, he's agreed to take on that role until her family can be located and notified. He offered to go to the hospital tonight."

"Did he say what's wrong with her?"

"They're still running tests, but they said she is showing symptoms of having overdosed on something. They don't know exactly what's wrong with her yet."

"Overdosed! What, like on drugs or something?"

"Could be, I suppose."

She checked her watch. "Aaron, the afternoon is just about over. I don't need you for anything more today, so why don't you find Simon and see if he needs you. And if he doesn't, you can start reading *Romeo and Juliet*."

"Are you trying to get rid of me?"

She laughed lightly. "No, of course not. But I am rather tired, and I'd like to get a walk in before dinner."

"Oh, you like walking, do you?"

"I do. I find it clears my mind, and I feel so much better afterwards. And the exercise is good for my dog."

"What kind of dog?"

Her face lit up at the very thought of Rupert. "He's a corgi. The same kind of dog the Queen has, only mine's got three colors and hers only have two. Her dogs are red and white. Mine has a mainly black coat with red and white points. I bring him to work every now and then, so you'll meet him soon, I'm sure. Do you like dogs?"

After telling her he did, Aaron said good-night and left.

Charlotte entered a couple of reminders for tomorrow in her daybook, closed it, and switched off the desk lamp. The dress Lauren had tried on was still draped over the dressing screen, but Charlotte decided to leave it there and let Aaron deal with it in the morning. After one last look around to make sure everything was tidied away, she closed the door to her workroom and locked it.

Fifteen minutes later, she locked the door of her bungalow, and with Rupert on his leash, the two set off on the short walk into town.

Walkers Ridge had always depended on tourism, and now the tourists were starting to come back. The area had long been a popular destination for artists and musicians and was rediscovering and repositioning itself as a beacon for photographers, yoga enthusiasts, hikers, and antique collectors, as well as, because of its rich, fertile farmland, a Mecca for New York City foodies keen to experience the farm-to-table experience and devour vegetables so fresh they'd been in the ground or on the vine until the very morning they were served.

Bentley's Bistro featured daily specials showcasing local ingredients and served only craft beers from a Catskills brewery. Next door, the Upper Crust Bakery served warm croissants and freshly brewed specialty coffees, and further on down the street, an ice cream parlor offered homemade ice cream made with real cream from cows almost within walking distance. Boutiques sold vintage clothing like paisley-patterned peasant skirts and tie-dyed T-shirts, as well as handmade jewelry and candles. The heady smells of patchouli and incense wafted from some of the shops, and if you didn't know better, you'd think it was 1968 all over again.

But Charlotte paid no attention to the stores as she and Rupert trotted along the back streets of the town until they reached Helm Street, the main thoroughfare. She slowed down to a walk and a few minutes later arrived at her destination. She pushed open the door to the police station, conveniently located beside the town hall; both were made of brick that had been painted white.

"Hello, Gus," she said to the front-desk officer seated behind the glass screen. "Is he in?"

"Sure is. He's expecting you. Just knock and go on in."

She knocked on the office door and poked her head around it. Walkers Ridge Chief of Police Ray Nicholson looked up from his computer and, with a confident smile, came around the side of the desk and reached behind her to close the door.

"Afternoon, ma'am. What can I do for you?"

He was a couple of inches over six feet tall and well built. The definition of his biceps, visible even under his blue shirt, attested to hours in the gym lifting weights. His neatly trimmed dark hair was starting to grey at the temples, adding to his natural air of authority.

Charlotte put her arms around his neck, and he bent down and kissed her.

Chapter 7

Charlotte and Ray had met about six months ago, when she and Rupert had found a small white dog running loose on the village green. Unsure if it was lost or abandoned, but certain it was in distress, Charlotte had offered it a few of Rupert's dog treats, and not knowing what else to do, she had taken the dog to the nearby police station. Ray had seemed very interested in the dog's welfare and promised he would make sure the little fellow was cared for. He'd taken Charlotte's name and address for his report and two days later, when he just happened to be driving by the hotel, had dropped in to let her know the microchipped dog had been reunited with his relieved owner.

"Did he spend the night at the vet's?" Charlotte asked.

Ray shook his head and gave her a sheepish grin. "I think he found my sofa quite comfortable."

Charlotte laughed, and after a few minutes of easy conversation, Ray had invited her to meet for a coffee. They'd discovered they shared a love of films, especially 1940s and '50s noir, and really good coffee.

Ray had moved to Walkers Ridge from Pennsylvania. He'd applied for the police chief job as a career move, but he was also looking for a fresh start following an amicable divorce. Meeting Charlotte had been an unexpected bonus.

"Something happened at the hotel today," Charlotte said, after she'd settled into the chair across from his desk, with Rupert lying at her feet. "It may be nothing, but I thought you should know." She described finding Lauren barely conscious in her bedroom, how the ambulance had been called, and finished up by telling him that a hospital nurse had told Harvey Jacobs that an overdose of some kind was suspected.

"Overdose?" Ray asked.

"They aren't sure yet what's wrong with her. Still running tests, apparently. But you know, when I saw her, I wondered if it might be something like that. She was so unresponsive—exactly like what you read about in the papers when someone has overdosed."

"Did they say what kind of drug she might have taken?"

Charlotte shook her head. "If the nurse told him, Harvey didn't say. I suppose it could be something she took by mistake, but when you hear 'drug overdose,' you tend to think the worst, don't you?"

"You do." He thought for a moment. "Look, just to be on the safe side, I think I'll take a run over to the hospital and see what's going on. I'd send Phil, but he's out on a call. Will you be home later? I'll phone you."

Charlotte gathered up Rupert and stood up. "That would be great. I'd love to know what you find out. If you can tell me, that is."

"I'll tell you what I can," he replied as he also stood up. "Now, would you two like a ride home? It's on my way."

"No, we're fine. We want to complete our walk, don't we, Rupert?" The corgi raised his head slightly when he heard his name. Charlotte smiled at him and then turned to Ray. "Why don't I pick up a few groceries, and if you don't have other plans, you could come by later and we can talk over dinner."

"Sounds great. I'll call you and let you know when I'm on my way."

Half an hour later, pleasantly out of breath, Charlotte let herself and Rupert into their bungalow, set down her small bag of shopping, peeled off her dog-walking clothes, and headed for the shower. Ten minutes later, wrapped in a fluffy white towel with another one on her head, turban style, she made her way to her bedroom. She chose clean, comfortable pants and a green and white striped Ralph Lauren top that she'd bought on sale at a discount outlet. She was halfway to the kitchen to begin preparing dinner when her phone rang. It was Ray, telling her he'd be there in about forty-five minutes.

She put out Rupert's dinner and then seasoned the chicken breasts and put them in the oven while she prepared potatoes. Ray liked old-fashioned, plain cooking, and although she enjoyed good food, she wasn't much into cooking anymore. Keeping things simple suited her just fine.

This bungalow on the grounds of Jacobs Grand Hotel had been her home for the past ten years. It was small, but it suited her perfectly, reminding her of the old tied cottages that used to house workers on great English estates. The only difference was that she paid Harvey Jacobs a fair market-value rent.

She'd placed her table in front of the sitting-room window, with its beautiful view of the local river. The natural light was good, and although she rarely brought work home, if she had some detailed stitching to do, it was in front of this window that she did it.

The summer season at Jacobs Grand Hotel kept her busy, but in the downtime of winter, she supplemented her income by creating costumes for New York productions on a short-term contract basis. It was easy enough to catch the bus that picked up passengers at the village green and continued on, stopping at small towns along the way, all the way to the Port Authority Bus Terminal at Forty-Second Street. She loved days out in New York, the hustle of the city, the romance of the theater district, and the drive of the fashion district.

She finished setting the table, and a few minutes later, as Rupert's barking warned of an approaching vehicle, she lit a couple of candles. Footsteps crunched across the gravel, and she opened the door for Ray, letting in a cool blast of fresh spring evening air.

After kissing her, he took off his coat and went to wash his hands in the kitchen sink.

"Are you off duty now for the rest of the evening?" she asked over the sound of running water. He nodded. "Hungry?" He nodded again as he hung up the towel. "Like a glass of wine?"

"That sounds good," he replied.

"Dinner should be ready in a few minutes." She handed him a glass of white wine and sat beside him on the couch, tucking one leg under her as she turned toward him.

"Tell me," she said.

"Well, the good news is that Lauren has regained consciousness and is breathing on her own, but they wouldn't let me speak to her. She's not quite out of the woods yet but headed in the right direction. It was very lucky you found her when you did. The doctor said even five or ten minutes later and the outcome would most likely have been very different."

"Do they know what she took?"

"They did a tox screen but haven't got the results back yet. I hope to know more when we're able to talk to her."

He took a sip of wine.

"Now it's your turn to tell me," he said. "You said you thought something didn't seem quite right when you found Lauren. What did you mean by that?"

"She seemed so limp and well, just out of it. I wondered if she'd taken something."

"A suicide attempt, you mean?"

Charlotte nodded. "I had a cousin who tried to kill herself. My aunt found her passed out, and what she described looked a lot like Lauren."

She glanced at Rupert lying beside them and then bent over and gave the fur on his back a friendly rub.

"But I wouldn't have thought Lauren was the type to try to commit suicide. Of course, you can never really know what's going on in someone's mind, but she didn't seem depressed or unhappy to me. Quite the opposite, in fact. She seemed very confident that she was on her way to bigger and better things."

"But suicide attempts aren't always what they seem," Ray said. "Sometimes people do it to attract attention or to send a message to someone. You know—'If you break up with me, I'll kill myself, and you'll be sorry.'"

Charlotte glanced up at him.

"I offered to ride in the ambulance to the hospital with Lauren," she remarked as she straightened up, "but the paramedic said only family can do that. It occurred to me that Lauren didn't take anything with her, so I thought I'd go back to her room tonight and choose a few items that she'll need while she's in hospital. A bit of makeup, her own nightdress, that sort of thing."

"That's a good idea," said Ray. "I'm sure she'd appreciate your thoughtfulness. We can walk over together after dinner."

The oven timer dinged to let them know the chicken was done. Charlotte mashed the potatoes, and they worked together to plate the meal. Charlotte closed the curtains against the night while Ray set the plates on the table and Rupert kept a close eye on everything.

Ray looked thoughtful as he piled mashed potatoes on his fork.

"Do you know if her room is locked now?" he asked.

"It wasn't locked this morning when I found her, but I don't know if someone locked the door after she was taken to hospital."

He helped himself to a few more buttered carrots.

*

"This is her room, number fifteen here on the right," Charlotte said in a stage whisper as the two made their way along the hotel's second-floor corridor. They tried the door, and it opened. After closing it softly behind them and locking it, Ray flicked on the light switch by the door and then pulled a small a flashlight out of his pocket and shone it around the room.

"You'd be surprised how much better you can see with one of these, even with overhead lighting," he said in response to Charlotte's quizzical look. The beam picked out the details of small things on the dresser: a little cut-glass dish containing a couple of pairs of dangly silver earrings and two quarters, a photo of a dark-haired woman holding a small dog, and several hair clips.

"It's just the bedroom, is it?" he asked. "No bathroom?"

"She'd have used the communal one down the hall," Charlotte said. She opened a bureau drawer and flipped through a few neatly folded sweaters and selected one.

She picked up a cell phone on the bedside table and showed it to Ray, who nodded.

"I'm sure she'd be glad to have that. What else do you think she'd like?"

"Probably some underclothes, sleepwear, toiletries, makeup. When she's feeling better, she'll definitely want to tidy herself up a bit. Oh, and we'd better send some street clothes so she'll have something clean to wear home. Jeans and a sweater. And maybe a—"

"Where's her purse?" Ray interrupted. "We haven't seen her purse. Where would she be likely to keep it?"

"Could the ambulance people have picked it up and taken it with them?"

"Possibly, if there was time. Though I expect the paramedics' priority was preparing her for transport and getting her on her way as soon as possible."

Charlotte opened the door of the small closet and checked the floor. "It's not here. Usually a woman sets it down someplace where it's easy to get at, so you'd expect it to be beside the little table or maybe by the bed or on the table." She pointed to a small table, painted white, with a straight-backed, uncomfortable-looking chair in front of it.

"I'll call the hospital and ask the nurse to check for it. Her room's been left unlocked, so we want to make sure her bag hasn't been stolen," said Ray.

He surveyed the room with an experienced eye.

"Well, I don't think there's anything more to see here. Doesn't look as if anything's out of place. Let's just gather up a few things for her and be on our way."

Charlotte took a closer look at the rumpled bed where she had found Lauren. The bedding gave off a sour smell, and she thought she saw a damp patch on the coverlet.

"Ray, this bed needs changing. We can't leave it like that. It should be nice for her when she returns. I'll ask the housekeeper to take care of it tomorrow."

Charlotte lifted the pillow to reveal a pair of pajama bottoms printed with a pink sheep pattern and a pink T-shirt.

"There's a bag on the floor of her closet that's probably for laundry. We'll put these in there and see if we can find another bag to use for the things we want to bring to the hospital." As she picked up the nightclothes, something fell to the floor. She bent over and retrieved a bright red box with the name "Garrard" on it.

"Oh my," she said, turning to Ray and showing him the box. "Look at this."

"What is it?"

"It's a Garrard jewelry box." She snapped the lid open to reveal a ring set with a large blue stone surrounded by what looked like diamonds. She held it out to him, and he shone his flashlight on it as he peered at it. "If this is real, it's worth thousands," she said. "The box isn't new, though. You can see it's a little faded and frayed around the edges. This could be an heirloom or auction piece."

"Now where would Lauren get something like that?"

Charlotte thought for a moment. "I think it's likely this was a gift. I certainly can't see her buying something like this for herself, can you? How could she possibly afford it? And as Garrard was the royal jeweler for centuries, I'd say this was almost certainly a gift from a British admirer."

Chapter 8

A light, steady rain dripping from the black branches of bare trees made a soft, mournful sound as Ray and Charlotte trudged along the path that led from the back door of the hotel. Ray paused to listen to raised voices coming from Brian Prentice's bungalow. The lights were on, but the curtains were drawn.

"Who's in there?" he asked.

"Brian Prentice and his wife. He's this year's special guest star, and yes, he's from the U.K."

"Do you think he could have given her that ring?"

"I wouldn't put it past him," Charlotte replied. "Giving a girl he barely knows a ring like that is just the sort of over-the-top thing he would do. So pathetic."

"Why do you say that?"

"They haven't known each other very long, so if he did give her that ring, he must be desperate."

They walked on in silence, and then, just as they reached Charlotte's bungalow, she reached out and touched Ray on the arm. "I've just had a thought. What if Brian didn't give that ring to her? What if she stole it from his wife, Lady Deborah? Deborah's the daughter of an earl, and the family owns some pretty stunning jewelry, or so I've read, although whether she'd have any of it here with her, I wouldn't know. Well, she wouldn't have all of it; she'd have left at least some of it at home, in the bank. That's where most women keep their tiaras and such like." She laughed. "Not that I do myself, of course."

"There is another possibility," said Ray as they took off their boots and damp coats.

"What's that?" asked Charlotte as she poured water into the coffee maker.

"It's possible," said Ray, "that someone put the ring there. Her door was unlocked, so anyone could have come in and planted it or just hidden it." He walked over to the couch and sat down, taking the box out of his pocket and setting it on the coffee table. "Although I can't think of a reason anyone would want to do that." After a moment, he asked, "Does the hotel owner live on the premises?"

"He does," Charlotte said. "Harvey and his wife have a rather nice apartment in the main building. Their nephew, Aaron, my new assistant, is staying with them. Why?"

"I'd like you to call him, tell him we've been in Lauren's room to collect a few things for her, and ask him to lock the room. But don't mention the ring. I couldn't have left it in an unlocked room and it'll be safer with me."

"I'll call him now. Either he'll do it himself or send someone to do it."

"Is there a caretaker?"

"There's a couple who live in Walkers Ridge who work here. She does the housekeeping, helps out in the kitchen when needed, and he does the odd jobs and repairs around the place. There's always something that needs doing. In the old days, there would have been ten men doing his work—gardening, painting, cleaning out the gutters, unplugging sinks . . . all the never-ending jobs that you've got to stay on top of."

She called the Jacobs' apartment, exchanged a quick greeting with Aaron, and then asked to speak to his uncle. She repeated what Ray had asked her to tell him and then said good-night and hung up.

"I just remembered something," she said. "I didn't pursue it at the time, but now it's got me wondering."

Ray raised a rather handsome eyebrow.

"Aaron said something to the effect that he was surprised his uncle would give Lauren a job. So he must have known her from somewhere before and didn't think too much of her."

"Why don't I leave that with you?" Ray said. "Ask Aaron what he can tell you about her." He stifled a yawn. "That coffee's just what I needed," he said. "I hope the caffeine kicks in soon."

When they'd finished their drinks, Ray sighed and checked his watch.

"I'm going to have to go back to the hospital tonight and ask someone to check Lauren's locker to see if her purse is there. I'll leave that bag of personal things for her so she'll have them in the morning. By then, I hope she'll be well enough to talk to us."

Charlotte showed him to the door. He held her, kissed her, and then let her go. "Be sure to lock the door behind me," he said.

"Why? Do you think there's danger lurking?"

"There's always danger lurking. And anyway, I'm a policeman. Telling people to lock their doors is part of what I do, and my job would be a whole lot easier sometimes if everybody just did as I asked."

He gave her a cheery wave, and with a light smile, she locked the door behind him. An hour later, after Rupert was settled in for the night and just as she was starting to think about getting ready for bed, her phone rang. It was Ray.

"Her purse isn't at the hospital. Will you please keep an eye out for it tomorrow?"

"And what about the ring?" Charlotte asked.

"I'll lock it in our safe until we can return it to its owner."

Whoever the rightful owner might be, thought Charlotte.

Chapter 9

The overnight rain had washed away almost all the remaining snow, leaving only dirty patches at the bases of the trees that lined the pathway to the main building and on the grounds where the bungalows were located. Spring had officially arrived, and this morning a light, refreshing breeze was blowing along the river, bringing with it a sweet hint of warmer days to come. Even this early in the day, the sun had an intensity that hadn't been there just a couple of weeks earlier.

Charlotte let herself into the hotel through the staff entrance and walked along the corridor that led to the backstage area. Beyond that, down another short passageway, were her workroom and the costume storage area. As she passed the black curtains that made up the theater wings, a man's voice caught her attention. She stopped to listen.

"Look, Brian, what you get up to in your own time is your business, but when it starts affecting your ability to remember your lines, be on time for rehearsals, or work with the rest of the cast, then as the director, it becomes my problem. You've got to lay off the booze. It's destroying your career. Or what's left of it."

Feeling uncomfortable at overhearing Brian get a dressing down, Charlotte was about to move on. But she decided she wanted to hear what Brian Prentice had to say in response, so she ducked out of the corridor and stood between the curtains where she wouldn't be seen by anyone who might come down the hallway. It was still a few minutes before nine, and she guessed that the rest of the cast on call for this rehearsal would start to arrive in a few minutes.

"Well, I'm not late this morning, am I?" Brian said, finally.

"No, but I can smell the booze on you from last night. It's not pleasant, and you don't look too clever," said Simon Dyer.

"Going through a bad patch right now, you see," Brian said. "Deborah's about to leave me, I know she is. I don't even know why she agreed to come here with me. The only reason I can think of is that she liked the idea of being so close to New York City. And then I did a really stupid thing that probably means I pressed the self-destruct button. When Deborah finds out, I'll be for the high jump. She'll have my guts for garters this time, for sure."

"What have you done?" Simon asked. "Do you want to tell me? Is it something I can help with?"

"Nah."

"The thing is, Brian, this is a funny old place. For some of us—you and me, for example—it's our last chance to make something of ourselves so our careers don't end in the gutter. For others, it's a starting point. For them, the only way from here is up. The ones just out of theater school are paying their dues here, and it's up to us to show them the ropes." He waited, and when there was no response, he continued. "Think about it this way, Brian. These young actors will take what happens here this summer with them for the rest of their careers. Do you really want your legacy to be 'the old drunk British geezer I worked with that summer in the Catskills'? Because if you don't clean up your act, that's exactly where you're headed."

The only reply was a deep, violent coughing fit that sounded as if a pair of lungs were about to be turned inside out.

"And Brian, you might want to do something about the smoking. It's destroying that beautiful voice of yours. Look, I'm sorry if all this sounds harsh," Simon continued, "but someone needs to talk to you like a Dutch uncle, and I guess that someone had to be me. Okay. Speech over. Let's get ready for the rehearsal. I need and expect full participation from you this morning. You're the company's lead actor, and I'm looking to you to lead the company."

"What about Lauren?"

"What about her?"

"Well, will somebody be standing in for her?"

"Of course."

"Have you, er, heard how she's doing?"

"I had a message from Harvey this morning. I'm planning to update the cast in a few minutes."

Just as they finished speaking, footsteps behind Charlotte signaled approaching cast members, so she slipped out from behind the curtain and, at a quick pace, hoping to give the impression she'd just arrived, bustled toward Simon. She was relieved that Brian had moved away and was standing alone in the middle of the stage, looking out at the empty seats. A young actor approached him, and the two were soon in animated conversation. Brian raised his arm in a sweeping gesture, pretending to take off his hat and then bow. His movements were fluid and expressive. If they seemed exaggerated on stage, they would read beautifully from the audience. A moment later, the younger man took a step back, repositioned his feet slightly wider apart, and lifted his arm. Brian grasped it and lifted it higher. The actor then bent his knees and mimicked Brian's bow. Brian gave him a reassuring pat on the shoulder, and the young man smiled at him and then joined the other cast members.

Simon and Charlotte turned to each other.

"Morning, Simon."

"Hello, there." He tipped his head in Brian's direction. "That was interesting."

"Brian always was generous with other actors. Makes sure they have their moment and never tries to upstage. He's also really good with the stagecraft. Makes it look so easy."

"You know him, do you?"

"Yes, we worked together at the RSC a long time ago."

"I wondered if your paths might have crossed."

"Well," said Charlotte, "I just wanted to remind you that we're going to need all the cast members in for measurements and then fittings. I'd like Aaron to work with me on this, so we can get the costumes sorted in half the time. We can work around your rehearsal schedule."

Simon nodded. "Sounds good. Thanks for the reminder. We'll start booking them in at the end of the week."

"Fortunately, we took Lauren's measurements yesterday and started on her dresses, so as soon as she returns . . ."

"If she returns," Simon said.

"Oh, gosh, is it that bad? I thought she was on the mend, and just assumed . . ."

"Look, I'm just about to brief the cast. Why don't you stay for that?"

"I'd like that very much. I'd also like to say a few words to them, if you don't mind," said Charlotte.

"No problem."

In the center of the stage, a young actor was arranging chairs in a semicircle. Once the rest of the cast had arrived, one or two with hair still damp from the shower and several clutching coffee cups, Simon clapped his hands to get their attention.

"All right, everybody. Take your seats, please. I want to give you an update on how Lauren's doing, and then I want to introduce you to our costume designer."

They shuffled to the chairs and settled quickly amidst an air of expectation. Usually the conversational hubbub would die down slowly, but this morning, they immediately gave their director their full attention.

"Harvey Jacobs called me this morning. He's been in touch with the hospital, and they're keeping him informed about Lauren's condition. The good news is that she's out of danger, but the bad news is that she's experiencing some medical issues. They're still not sure what happened, but it seems likely she took an overdose of something."

One or two cast members gasped, raising their hands to cover their mouths. A few exchanged quick glances of surprise.

"So if any of you have any information or know anything at all about what might have happened to her, come and see me."

"Is she coming back?" one of the older actresses asked.

"That's a good question. It's a little too early to say," Simon responded carefully. "We hope so. If she can recover in time, she will be back. If not, unfortunately, she'll have to be replaced. In the meantime, we go ahead with rehearsals, with someone standing in for her."

He waited for a moment to give the cast time to digest what they had just been told. "Does anyone have any questions?" His eyes scanned the group. "No? Well if there's nothing else, let me introduce you to Charlotte Fairfax, who is our costume designer and wardrobe supervisor rolled into one. Charlotte has a lot of experience, including the Royal Shakespeare Company in Stratford-upon-Avon, so you're in very good hands." He gestured in her direction, and Charlotte stood up.

"Good morning, everyone." She glanced at their faces, but deliberately avoided making eye contact with Brian, although she could feel his eyes on her. "I haven't met all of you yet, but I will as soon as we begin costume fittings at the end of the week and, er, I'm looking forward to that." She could feel her composure evaporating under Brian's gaze but plowed on.

"I've been asked to tell you that Lauren's handbag—that is, her purse—seems to be missing. Please keep your eyes open for it. I don't know what it looks like, but if you find a woman's bag, it'll probably be hers. If you do find a woman's bag, please don't open it or disturb the contents—just bring it to me in the costume department." She started to sit down and then quickly straightened up. "We're located just down the hall, on the other side of the back entrance."

Chapter 10

The door to the wardrobe department was wide open, and Aaron was waiting for her when she arrived at her office a few minutes later.

"Morning, Charlotte. I made you a tea."

"Thanks, Aaron. I could murder a cup." Charlotte picked up the mug and surveyed her workroom as she took her first sip. "I'm pretty sure I locked up last night. How did you get in this morning?"

"After my uncle spoke to you last night, he sent me down to lock up Lauren's room, then told me to hang on to the keys. Said I should have access to the rooms and backstage areas. So I just let myself in this morning. Hope that was all right."

"Oh, I see. No, that's fine. Just wanted to make sure my mind wasn't playing tricks on me. Or that someone else hadn't been in here trying to steal our fabrics. Right, well, the cast will be coming in later this week to start fittings, so we need to get ready for them. What about that spreadsheet you suggested for keeping track of their roles and plays? Could you work on that today?"

Aaron nodded and took out his laptop. "I'll do it on here." He pointed at Charlotte's elderly, enormous desktop computer. "If I were you, I'd take everything off that you want to keep. If you can. There might not even be a port for a USB drive. I'm surprised that dinosaur still works. Do you ever use it?"

"Not very often," Charlotte admitted. "It takes all morning just to warm up, and when it's finally up and running, it can't do very much. You're right. There may be old inventory information stored on it, so why don't you check it out, copy anything you think might be useful, and then we might as well scrap it. It's just taking up space."

She gave him an encouraging smile. "You might just be the breath of fresh air we so desperately need around here."

She pointed at the dressing screen. "Juliet's act-one dress. We won't make any alterations until we know if Lauren's going to rejoin the cast, so you can put it back in wardrobe storage for now." Aaron stood up, taking his coffee with him.

"No, no!" she cried. "All food and drinks must stay well away from the costumes, fabrics, worktables. I wasn't at all happy when Lauren left that open can of energy drink on the worktable, but I didn't want to say anything to her about it, although I should have. A spilled drink can ruin a garment. We can't risk it. I thought they would have taught you that at your fancy design school."

He set the coffee down with a sheepish, apologetic grin. "They probably did and I forgot. It makes sense."

"Did they also mention hand washing? Did you know the embroiderers who worked on the royal wedding dress washed their hands every thirty minutes and changed their needles every three hours to keep everything pristine?"

"I did not know that," said Aaron.

"And be careful when you lift the dress off the screen. *Lift* being the operative word. Use both hands. Don't drag it. If you do, you risk snagging it. And for some reason, it's easier to retrieve it off the same side of the screen as it was placed, so go round the back."

He disappeared behind the screen, and a moment later, the dress was gone. He reappeared with it draped over his right arm and carrying a black purse in his left hand.

"Look what I found," he said, holding the bag up and away from his body. Charlotte groaned and gave her forehead a little smack.

"Of course! I should have thought. It'll be Lauren's. Here, give it to me. The police are looking for that bag."

Aaron's eyebrows shot up and he frowned. "They are? Why?"

"Simon told the cast this morning that she'd had an overdose of something, but they're not sure yet what it was, or how or why." She shrugged. "They don't know much yet. I'd have thought your uncle would have told you all this. He called the hospital last night and they told him."

She took the bag from him.

"Are you going to open it?" he asked.

"Just to check and make sure it's hers."

The bag was an ordinary Michael Kors tote bag. Not wildly expensive, but with its gold fob and tassel, it was nice enough. Charlotte unzipped it, peered inside, and retrieved a small wallet. She opened it and examined a New York State driver's license. She pursed her lips, made a little noise, and then read out the name on the license: "Leah Patricia Kaplan."

"That's her," said Aaron. "Lauren Richmond's just her stage name."

"Tell me about her," Charlotte said. "You mentioned yesterday that you didn't understand how your uncle could have hired her. What did you mean by that? How do you know her?"

"We knew her in high school," Aaron replied. "She was in the same class as my cousin. She, Leah that is, was the leader of the mean girls. Picked on other girls they didn't like. Girls who were better looking or younger and smarter than they were. They singled out my cousin and they made her life a living hell. They bullied her to death, really. She stopped going to school, kept herself in her room, but still they kept on at her. In the end, she killed herself."

"Oh, Aaron, that's terrible. I'm so sorry to hear this. I don't know what to say, but it must have been awful for your family. So she was your cousin, but she wasn't Harvey's daughter, so how . . ."

"There are two sisters and a brother. Uncle Harvey, my mother, and my Aunt Esther. My cousin was Aunt Esther's daughter. Her only child, in fact."

"And how long ago did this happen?"

"Nine years ago. She was only fourteen."

"I see. And Harvey, did he know that about this Lauren? Sorry, I think of her as that. Leah."

"No. He didn't make the connection, but there's no reason, really, why he should have. My uncle doesn't hire the actors. He leaves casting decisions and things like that to the director. I doubt if he could even tell you any of the actors' names. I tried talking to him about her last night, but I didn't pick the right time. I could try talking to him again.

"But the worst thing is that Leah was never punished for what she did. She just got on with her life. She gets to have a career and probably doesn't even know what happened to my cousin, and if she did, she wouldn't care."

Neither said anything for a moment, and then Aaron resumed speaking.

"I hate her. I hate everything about her. I'll try to be professional around her, of course, but I wanted to ask if you would look after her fittings. I don't want to touch her." He looked with distaste at the dress she had tried on. "It's hard enough just touching something she's worn. You talk about hand washing. Makes me want to do just that."

"Does she know who you are, Aaron? Your family, I mean?"

"I doubt it. My aunt has a married name. My cousin's last name wasn't Jacobs."

"Oh, that's such a sad story. I'm so sorry about your cousin," said Charlotte. "I understand how you feel about the dress, so just leave it there and I'll deal with it. And I'll look after her, too, if she comes back. But I'd better let the police know her bag's been found."

She slipped the wallet back in the handbag and phoned Ray while Aaron opened the box that contained the costume details. He pulled out a card and studied it as Charlotte told Ray she'd checked the wallet and discovered Lauren's real name. Keeping her tone neutral, she shifted slightly in her chair as she felt Aaron's eyes upon her. As she listened to Ray, she met Aaron's intense gaze full on. He had stopped the pretense of looking at a card and was looking at her with an odd look on his face that she read as a mixture of fear and embarrassment.

"Oh, that's interesting," Charlotte said, still looking at Aaron. "Right. I'll let them know. See you later."

She ended the call and then turned to Aaron. "It seems Lauren is attracting a bit of media attention. Someone called the local newspaper to tell them she's in hospital. So you'd better find Simon and let him know and also tell your uncle. If the papers pick up the story, they'll probably want to interview one or both of them, so they should start thinking about what they want to say if a reporter calls."

Well, well, thought Charlotte, after Aaron had left on his mission. Who could have alerted the media? Lauren's agent, if she'd had one? Lauren was ambitious, and it made sense that she would seek publicity, and the more the better, to fulfill her ambition and advance her career. Could Lauren have taken an overdose of something just to attract media attention?

Or perhaps Harvey Jacobs had told the press. The hotel could benefit nicely from the publicity and the increased bookings it would likely generate.

Who else? Brian Prentice? She wouldn't put anything past him. His sagging career might get a temporary boost from being a bottom-line mention in a newspaper story, but it seemed his career was long past its "best before" date. Unless he quit drinking, she didn't see a second-act rebound in his future.

And what if the attention on Lauren brought their affair to light? That could really backfire on him with Lady Deborah. If Brian was the one who'd notified the paper, had he thought through the potential ramifications?

Unless, of course, he was aiming at the British tabloids, which would make a proper meal of this scandal: "Once-Famous Actor Husband of British Aristocrat Caught in Affair With American Actress Less Than Half His Age" would make a terrific headline.

And what about Aaron? Young sir had looked decidedly uncomfortable while she was talking to Ray. She couldn't see how he would benefit from any publicity, and she doubted he had informed the media, but he certainly had a good reason to dislike Lauren and had admitted he hated her. Could he have been involved in some way in what happened to Lauren?

She shook off that thought and took a sip of her now tepid tea while she tried to knit together these tangled strands of speculation. But what if publicity was the second step in someone's plan? And to get things to that point, what if the first step had been to make Lauren very ill?

Chapter 11

After ending the conversation with Charlotte, Ray, too, had mulled over various possibilities while reminding himself to keep his theorizing in check. A ping signaling a priority e-mail interrupted his thoughts, and after reading it, he called Charlotte back.

"When we were in her room last night, did you see any Tylenol?" He listened for a moment and then asked, "Can you take another look in her purse?" After letting her know he was on his way over, he put on his coat and hat and closed the office door behind him.

"Come on, Phil," he said to the sergeant sitting at the desk nearest to his office. "We're going over to Jacobs Hotel to pick up the purse that belongs to that actress who's in the hospital. Just had the tox screen results. She's had an overdose of acetaminophen."

"Acetamino . . ."

"Phen. Tylenol. Plain old Tylenol."

Phil Davenport was a lanky, easygoing kind of guy, often underestimated by young offenders who made fun of his curly red hair. But when pushed, he turned quickly into someone they really shouldn't mess with.

"When we've got the purse, I want you to go to the hospital and see if she's up to speaking with you. I'm starting to get a feeling that something's not right here, and we need to get to the bottom of it," said Ray as he slid into the passenger seat and buckled his seat belt.

They drove along Helm Street, waving at the owner of the antique shop who was setting up an old-fashioned English pram with a sign around it as part of his sidewalk display.

"Things don't change much around here, do they, Ray?" said Phil. "Do you ever long for more action, more big-city kind of crime?"

"Yeah, sometimes," said Ray. "It would be good to have a chance every now and then to practice what we learn at those courses the state sends us on. 'Advanced crowd control' and what have you. Crowd control hasn't been needed in these parts since 1969. How about you? Ever think you'd like to move to the big city?"

Phil smiled. "Sometimes, but it ain't gonna happen. The wife wants the kids to grow up in a nice, safe community where everybody knows everybody else, and nothing ever happens."

"Can't blame her, really," said Ray, as they turned into the hotel driveway. "If I had kids, I'd probably want the same thing." He pointed to an almost empty unpaved parking area near the entrance. "Park over there. We'll go in the front door with our hats on. Makes our visit look more official."

The two officers walked up the short sidewalk to the hotel's front door and entered the lobby. It was empty. Overstuffed brown sofas and easy chairs waiting for occupants were positioned on an elaborately patterned brown carpet. Several huge jardinières overflowing with ferns whose brown leaves matched the furniture were dotted about. Straight ahead of them was a heavy wooden reception desk with a little silver bell and guest book. Phil dinged the bell, and a moment later, a door behind the desk opened and Harvey Jacobs presented himself.

"Oh," he said, peering from one to the other, "how may I help you gentlemen?"

"We've come to pick up something from Charlotte Fairfax," said Ray. "If you would please let her know we're here?"

"Yes, of course." Harvey picked up the phone on the desk, entered four digits, and waited. "Oh, Aaron, it's you. Is Charlotte there?" He listened for a moment. "No, just tell her I've got two police officers in reception to see her. They're here to pick something up."

He replaced the receiver. "If you'd like to have a seat, she'll be right with you."

"That's all right," said Phil. "We'll stand."

"Very good. Well, if you don't need me for anything else, I'll get back to my work." Jacobs disappeared back through the door, leaving Phil contemplating several rows of old-fashioned pigeon holes and dozens of room keys hanging from little hooks. He placed his forearm on the reception desk, leaned on it, and turned to Ray.

"I remember those days," he said in a low voice, "when you'd get your room key and then leave it at the desk when you went out so they'd know when the room was unoccupied. I didn't know hotels still had proper keys. Thought they all had swipe cards now."

"Apparently not," said Ray. He stiffened at the sound of approaching footsteps, and a moment later, Charlotte, carrying Lauren's black tote bag, trotted into the lobby. She smiled a hello at both of them and asked after Phil's family.

"I didn't really go through it," she said as she handed the bag to Ray. "Just checked the wallet to make sure it was hers. That's when I saw the different name. Leah Patricia Kaplan. Aaron told me she and her group of mean girls bullied his cousin to death about seven years ago."

"Jeez," said Ray. "Really? That's terrible."

"And I looked for the Tylenol, as you asked."

"Okay," said Ray. "Phil's going to take the bag over to the hospital now and see if Lauren's up to talking to him. She's the only one who can tell us what happened."

Charlotte said good-bye and disappeared back into the building as the two police officers left. When the lobby was empty, Harvey Jacobs remained where he was, his mind whirling, and then closed the little panel that served as the false back to a pigeonhole. This wasn't the first time he'd been grateful to his father for installing the peephole that let him see and hear what was going on at the reception desk and in the lobby without being observed.

*

"She's showing a lot of improvement this morning," said the nurse as she led Phil to Lauren's room. "In this type of situation, once the patient turns the corner, recovery can be very quick. Especially if she's young and fit and the amount of drug taken is below a certain threshold. She's very lucky, though, that she hasn't suffered any organ damage. In fact, after the doctor's finished his rounds, she could be discharged later today. We don't like to keep anyone in longer than necessary."

"Good to hear," said Phil. "Before we go in, could I just ask you a few questions about this Tylenol overdose?" The nurse answered his questions and then opened the door to Lauren's room. Phil followed her in and waited while she took Lauren's pulse. The nurse gave him a brief nod and then spoke to her patient.

"Sergeant Phil Davenport from our local police would like to ask you a few questions, Lauren, if you feel up to speaking with him."

"Sure."

"Don't be too long," the nurse said to Phil as she prepared to leave the room. "We don't want to tire her out." She lowered her voice and with her back to her patient, added, "If she shows any signs of distress, you should stop."

Lauren was wearing the pale yellow nightdress Charlotte had chosen for her that Ray had dropped off last night. She wriggled higher in the narrow bed with side rails to a sitting position, pulled the pillows up behind her, and then looked expectantly at Phil. He showed her the tote bag. "Yours?"

Lauren reached out for it. "Yeah."

"I'd like you to check and see if anything's missing."

Lauren opened it, scrabbled around examining the contents, and pulled out a zebra-patterned makeup bag. "Oh, thank God. I need this. You have no idea what it's been like."

She set it beside her on the bed and then went back to rummaging around in the tote bag. "No, everything seems to be here."

She picked up the makeup bag, unzipped it, and took out a lipstick and compact.

Phil pulled the visitor's chair closer to the bed and sat down. "Feel up to answering a few questions?" he asked as he flipped open his notebook.

"I already said yes. What would you like to know?" She clicked the clasp on the compact and examined her face in the mirror, turning it this way and that, to catch the light from the window that overlooked the front of the redbrick building.

"Apparently you've had an acetaminophen overdose. Most commonly found in the medication Tylenol. Do you remember taking Tylenol? Could you have exceeded the recommended dosage?"

Lauren shook her head. "I never take Tylenol. I don't even own any." She frowned. "The doctor asked me that question, too, and I was really surprised when he told me they'd found that drug in my system. Well, I know I didn't take it myself, so someone must have slipped it to me somehow. Trying to poison me, maybe. That's all I can think of."

"Okay. Now the nurse told me that someone with," he checked his notes, "acetaminophen toxicity can start feeling and showing symptoms anywhere from twenty-four to forty-eight hours after ingesting it. Can you think of any situation you were in up to two days before you felt ill during which time someone could have given you an excessive amount of the drug? Were you given any food or drink you didn't prepare yourself?"

"No, I don't remember anything like that."

"Well, I'll leave you to think about it. People some-times find it helpful to check their schedules to remind them where they were and what they were doing. See if you can come up with who you were with and what you were doing during that time period. Also think about anyone who might have wanted to harm you."

Lauren shook her head. "*Nooo*," she said slowly, with an ingratiating smile. "Why would anyone want to harm me?"

Phil, who had been briefed on Lauren's background, did not think it necessary to mention that the wife of a married man who is having an affair often harbors negative feelings toward the woman her husband is sleeping with.

He handed her his card, which she dropped into her tote bag without looking at it. "Well, if you do remember anything, no matter how trivial it might seem to you, please contact me. Thanks for your time today, and I hope you feel better soon."

"Oh, I'm feeling much better now," she said. "I'm anxious to get back to the theater. They said I might be discharged this afternoon."

She pulled a tube of foundation out of her makeup kit, squeezed a drop onto the end of her finger, and began dabbing at her face. It couldn't have been clearer that, as far as she was concerned, this interview was over. Phil got the message.

As he walked down the hall toward the elevator, he spotted a familiar figure hovering around the nurses' station. The fluorescent lighting meant he couldn't make out the details of the person, but he didn't need to. The unmistakable silhouette of a fedora with a belted raincoat could belong to none other than Fletcher Macmillan, general reporter for the *Hudson Valley Echo*, who, for want of staff, also served as its arts editor. He reviewed local art and photography exhibits, books by local authors, concerts, theater productions, and everything else of a cultural nature. Phil braced himself as Fletcher advanced toward him, notebook in hand. It wasn't the questions Phil minded; it was the New York accent, reminiscent of society characters in old black-and-white movies, combined with a pseudo-British vocabulary that really annoyed him. As far as Phil or anyone else knew, Fletcher had never been further east than Boston.

"Ah, Phil! The very fellow! I was going to ring you. Need a quote, if you'd be so kind. Were you here to see Lauren Richmond? Did she try to commit suicide? Or was she poisoned? What are the police doing about it? Should the rest of the community be concerned? Do we have a mad poisoner in our midst?"

"Tell you what, Fletcher," said Phil. "Give me a call at the office later today, and I'll have a proper statement for you. Let's do this right, shall we?" *Old chap*, he added to himself. A smile teased the corners of his mouth as he thought about Fletcher Macmillan interviewing Lauren Richmond. Both so ambitious and self-absorbed with a hugely overinflated sense of their own importance and talent. He snickered as he pressed the elevator button. He could hardly wait to read the story.

But first, he had to call Ray.

"We've got a problem," he said when Ray picked up. "A couple of them, actually. Lauren says she didn't take the Tylenol herself." He listened for a moment and then answered Ray's question. "Yes. I do believe her. And there's something else. Macmillan's sniffing around, and he used the same word Lauren did—*poison*."

Chapter 12

"Charlotte, Brian Prentice called while you were out." Aaron handed her one of her scrap pieces of paper with a number on it she could barely read. "He wants you to call him before four. He's at home in his bungalow."

Charlotte sighed and sat down at her desk. She'd dreaded this moment since Brian and his wife had driven past her on the day they arrived, and although she'd managed to avoid him when she spoke to the cast about Lauren's handbag, she knew she couldn't put off the inevitable much longer. She thought about sending Aaron off on an errand so she could return Brian's call in private, and then decided to grasp the bull by the horns.

"Aaron, I'm going over to the bungalow to speak with him. It's not even three o'clock, so I should be in time. You can hold the fort here."

She slipped on her green plaid spring coat and walked through the grounds to what was known as the "star bungalow." Simon had told her that Lady Deborah spent her days in New York City, lunching, visiting museums and galleries, usually returning late afternoon in time for a sherry before dinner. If her car was parked outside the bungalow, Charlotte would turn around and return to her office; if not, she and Brian could have their awkward meeting and get it over with. She doubted he'd been looking forward to it, either. She wondered if he'd known she would be here when he signed his contract to appear in this summer's productions. Still, everything between them had happened a long time ago, and he probably didn't care one way or the other about any of it now. Why should he? Come to that, why should she?

Lady Deborah's car was not there, so she knocked on the frame of the screen door.

"Come in, darling. It's open," Brian's voice called from the sitting room.

A feeling of discomfort surged through her. *Darling?* Obviously he was expecting someone else. She hurried back down the wooden steps. Feeling a little foolish but overcome by curiosity, she sidled over to the nearest tree and ducked behind it. At the sound of an approaching vehicle, she peered around the tree to see a taxi pulling up. Out of the taxi hopped Lauren, who paid the driver and then bounded up the short path to the bungalow. Then, apparently realizing someone might be watching, she slowed her pace, put one foot deliberately in front of the other and leaned heavily on the railing, hauled herself up the steps, and knocked on the door.

Brian opened the door and, in that silly, sly way of people who want to make sure they are not being observed, looked in both directions before closing the door.

Charlotte checked her watch. They'd have a good hour before Lady Deborah might be expected home. She toyed with the idea of waiting twenty minutes or so and then calling Brian on the number he'd left but decided that little prank was too childish.

She was surprised by how his turning up after all these years was resurrecting old memories she thought were well and truly buried. She hadn't seen him since that snowy November day in New York when he'd told her bluntly that their relationship was over.

"I've got something to tell you," he'd said. "I've met someone else. We're going to be married."

Stunned into disbelief, Charlotte had asked who the woman was.

"No one you know," Brian had replied with an apologetic smile that didn't quite mask the pride in his voice. "Her father is an earl."

First had come numbing shock, followed by unbearable emotional pain. They'd been together almost two years, and Charlotte loved the life they had created while they established their careers. The cozy little flat in Stratford-upon-Avon where they made love, cooked spaghetti dinners, and drank wine while they played

Scrabble late into the night. Her arm tucked through his as she rested her head on his shoulder at a midnight showing in a small art-house cinema. Strolling beside the timeless River Avon, holding hands, watching the sun come up. The excitement of opening nights and sweet sadness of strike parties, all with Brian—the up-and-coming golden boy of British theater.

Until the moment he'd actually told her they were finished, she'd had no idea he was seeing someone else. As her future collapsed, she found herself unable to board the London-bound plane with the rest of the company, and she'd decided to stay behind in New York for just another week or so while she pulled herself together. She couldn't bring herself to tell her parents what had happened, because putting it into words would make it true, but yes, she reassured them, she'd be home for Christmas.

But she wasn't. She spent the holiday alone in a shabby hotel room in the theater district, and on Boxing Day, she met a gay man in a coffee shop who turned out to be the dresser for a famous Hollywood actor who was appearing in a Eugene O'Neil play on Broadway. Sitting in a booth beside steamed-up windows, he'd listened to her story, hugged her, and offered to introduce her to a few friends who might be able to offer someone with her credentials a bit of contract work.

One thing had led to another, and step by step she created a life for herself in America.

Now, she took no pleasure in the fact that Brian was cheating on the woman he'd left her for. If they'll do it with you, they'll do it to you, as the saying goes.

Seeing what he'd become, or rather not become, she was relieved she hadn't married him, and she realized that all these years she'd been carrying a torch not for the man she'd had but for the man she wished she'd had.

Chapter 13

As Simon Dyer was about to call an end to the day's rehearsal, Charlotte Fairfax peered around the edge of a black velour curtain.

"Right," said Simon, catching sight of her. "That's it for today. We'll meet tomorrow morning and continue where we left off. Work on your lines tonight. Thanks, everybody."

The cast members gathered up their belongings and, chatting to one another, left the stage as Charlotte stepped onto it. Although there was a rehearsal room Simon could have used, for a variety of reasons he preferred to rehearse on an actual stage. He set his script on the prop table one of the actors had moved downstage to get out of the way during a fight scene.

"Hoped I'd find you still here," Charlotte said. "In case you haven't heard, Lauren has returned. I saw her arrive a few minutes ago."

Simon frowned. "Why wasn't I told? Christ, no one tells me anything around here. I'd better have a chat with her and see if she's going to be at rehearsal in the morning. Where is she now, do you know?"

"I just saw her going into the star bungalow."

Simon groaned and pointed at the front row of audience seating. "Let's sit down." He led the way down the short set of stairs that led from the stage to the floor of the theater, and then he turned around and held up a gentlemanly hand to help Charlotte down the steps.

"You know, Charlotte, sometimes I think you and I are the only grown-ups in the whole place. What the hell is Brian Prentice thinking?"

"I know what you mean. And I'm sorry, but I couldn't help but overhear the carpeting you gave him this morning about his drinking. When I knew him, he did drink too much, but in those days everyone just thought, 'Oh, that's an actor for you.' I mean, there was Peter O'Toole and Richard Burton. People took very little notice of it, really, but for him to think he can have an affair with Lauren under his wife's nose is just absurd. She's bound to find out, if she doesn't know already."

"Of course she knows. This can't be the first time. He's probably had so many of these little flings over the years, she must be well aware of the signs by now."

"Why would she settle for being treated like that, I wonder?" Charlotte said. "And from the likes of him, too. It's not as if he's fabulously wealthy. Or fabulously anything."

Simon laughed. "You could say the same thing about Lauren. What's in it for her? But she's probably flattered by the attentions of an older man. A few years from now, she'll look back on this and shudder. She's one of the most ambitious young actresses I've ever seen, but unfortunately for her, Brian's in no position to advance her career. He has no star power, no influence. No one's taken his phone calls for years. I hear that in London, people cross the street to avoid him. He still has lunch at the Ivy every now and then, and they always seat him at the back, out of the way. Sad, really."

"Oh, stop!" said Charlotte. "Keep that up and you'll have me feeling sorry for him. Still, in this business, there's a huge expectation for actors to keep up appearances. You know that. You have to appear to be successful and in demand if you want to get hired. You have to look young. It's part of the illusion. And as for Brian, he's behaving like such an idiot. The best thing he's got going for himself is an aristocratic wife—gives him a cachet that no else has—and why he would risk losing that I don't know. I'm sorry, but I just don't get it."

Simon shook his head. "I don't either. I wonder why she even came to New York with him. And this," he made an airy gesture taking in their surroundings, "doesn't really seem like the place for her. You'd think she'd be more at home in a suite at the Pierre than in a, let's face it, shabby bungalow in the grounds of a down-at-heel Catskills resort."

"I wondered about that, too. It makes no sense."

Simon took a sip from his water bottle.

"Simon, there's something else I've been wondering about this afternoon. About Lauren. Did you know she'd taken an overdose of Tylenol?"

"No, I hadn't heard that."

"Well," continued Charlotte, "here's what I'm wondering. What if she didn't take it herself but was somehow given it? And the thing is, I've been reading about Tylenol poisoning on the Internet, and it damages the liver. So if your liver is already damaged, from heavy drinking, say, the results can be fatal. So what if the Tylenol wasn't meant for her?"

"But it was meant for . . ."

"Brian," they chorused.

They were silent for a moment as the implication sunk in, and then Simon spoke. "Wow. That's heavy."

*

"Time you weren't here, darling." Brian Prentice buttoned his shirt and poured himself a drink. "First one today," he said. "I'd offer you one, but it's really time you were off." Lauren snuggled against him, but when he didn't respond, she stood up. "I'll miss you, love," he said. "Why don't you come back tomorrow? I've got a late call."

"I'll have to see what Simon has in mind for me. He doesn't know I'm back yet."

Having come straight from the hospital with no coat, she left wearing only the jeans and cheerful coral-colored sweater Charlotte had chosen for her. The late-afternoon sun was starting to slip behind the hills, sending a scattering of slanted rays through the skeleton branches of the trees as she strode down the path to the road that led to the hotel. Lauren crossed her arms and hugged herself in a warming gesture against the wind. As she crossed the road, the hum of a car's engine motoring up the drive urged her on. A moment later, she opened the back door, relieved to step into the welcoming warmth of the hotel.

Lady Deborah steered the car into the parking spot in front of the bungalow and switched off the ignition. She remained where she was for a moment before reaching for her handbag.

That was a little too close for comfort, thought Brian Prentice as his wife's footsteps on the stairs signaled her approach. He topped up his glass to calm his nerves.

"Come in darling. It's open."

*

Lauren unlocked the door to her bedroom and entered. After a quick look around, her first impression was that the place had been cleaned and tidied, and apparently someone had gone to the trouble to change the bedding. The ugly, dusty rose candlewick bedspread had been replaced with a new, pale yellow one. But she felt no gratitude toward whoever had done this for her. It was the least they could do for someone who'd been so sick.

Now that she was back, she had a lot to think about. That policeman's questions were troubling her, and she couldn't get them out of her head. Where had she been and what had she been doing in the forty-eight hours before she got sick? Who could have made her so sick that she'd almost died?

She kicked off her shoes and stretched out on the narrow bed. *Let's see.* There'd been that argument, she'd gone for a costume fitting, she'd spoken to Brian backstage, had her meals in the staff canteen as usual . . . nothing out of the ordinary. But if someone had given her an overdose of Tylenol—and apparently someone had—she couldn't work out how or when it had happened.

She turned on her side and yawned. A dull, heavy feeling was tugging at her eyelids, and she felt dangerously overcome with fatigue. Maybe a little nap before dinner . . . she'd just close her eyes for a minute or two. It had probably been a mistake to go and see Brian when she'd just been released from hospital. Maybe it hadn't been such a good idea getting involved with him. It had to end sometime, and now might be a good time to dump him, so she could concentrate on preparing for the upcoming season. Maybe try a little harder on the publicity side. She'd got all she was going to get out of poor old Brian anyway—some good acting tips and a nice ring.

Her eyes flew open. How could she have forgotten about the ring? She raised herself to a sitting position and yanked the bedspread off the pillow. She lifted the pillow. Nothing. She placed her hand between the top and bottom sheet, smoothing them. She sank back. Of course. The bedding had been changed, so whoever changed the bed must have found the little red box with the ring in it. Maybe it was on the dresser. She got up and examined every surface in the room. Nothing. She pulled out drawers and rooted around but didn't find it. With a furiously pounding heart, she sat down on the bed to think.

*

Dinner in the canteen was a low-key affair. People who always ate together had staked out specific tables, while others liked to seek out different companions to vary the conversation. Still others, happy with the quiet company of a book or magazine, preferred to keep to themselves. And there was a clear, unspoken understanding that anyone reading a script or a Shakespeare text was to be left strictly alone.

For those with bungalow accommodation—Brian Prentice and Lady Deborah, Charlotte, and Simon Dyer—canteen meals were optional. When she was too tired to cook or hadn't done her grocery shopping, Charlotte ate there, although she found the food oversalted and on the stodgy side. You could pile on a lot of weight in no time in a place like that, if you weren't careful.

The staff canteen had been roped off so only a small seating section was open in the off season. It operated in the usual institutional cafeteria style, with a straight serving line incorporating both self-serve for salads and desserts and a woman in a white uniform dishing up the hot entrees. The choice was always limited to a vegetarian meal or a home-style dinner.

The company was well into their meatloaf with mashed potatoes and corn or vegetarian pizzas when Lauren made her entrance. She paused in the doorway long enough for everyone to see her and the effect of her presence to register. Heads swiveled in her direction as conversations tailed off and the room became silent. Simon Dyer stood up and began to clap, and some of the company joined in with a smattering of halfhearted, polite applause. Simon walked over to her, gave her a perfunctory hug, and then spoke to her.

Charlotte shot Aaron a glance filled with understanding concern as Simon approached their table with Lauren. She gave Aaron a quick nod and gestured at his plate, and for the benefit of those seated at tables close enough

Chapter 14

"All right, if I could just have everybody gather round," said Simon a few days later in his authoritative, directorial voice as the cast members waited on stage to start the day's rehearsal. "Today we continue with *Romeo and Juliet*, act two, scene one. The balcony scene. One of my favorites, and by the time we're finished with this, I hope it'll be one of your favorites, too.

"So Peter, let's have you a little more upstage center," Simon moved the actor playing Romeo toward the back of the stage, "and Lauren, somewhere we've got a little pretend balcony for you that will do for now. In the actual production, you'll be higher up."

He stopped speaking to the assembled actors and spoke in a lower voice to Aaron, who was working with him this morning.

"I want you to open the backdrop curtain just enough so we can see Lauren. And then place the little balcony in the gap for her to stand on. You'll find it somewhere back there." He gestured toward the loading dock area. "And when you've done all that, come back and stay close to me in case I need you." Aaron flew off, and a few minutes later, the curtains parted about six feet and a large box with a handrail along the side facing the audience and a couple of steps on the opposite side for mounting was pushed on stage.

"This is an important scene," Simon said to the cast, "so I'd like everyone except Peter and Lauren to leave the stage. And I don't want you backstage talking. I want you all to take a seat in the audience anywhere you like and just watch and listen. Spread yourselves out, and let's have a few of you at the back. Maybe you'll learn something, and it'll be helpful for Peter and Lauren to have some live bodies to act for. And as for you, Peter and Lauren, I want projection. Your audience members will hold up their hands if they can't hear you. You need to start getting a sense of the space and what you need to do to be heard in the back row.

"Right. Here we go. Lauren, use the crossover area to take your position on the balcony before the scene starts. You'll actually be there, but dark, while Peter says his opening line: 'He jests at scars that never felt a wound.' Then, we'll use spotlighting to reveal you. His opening line is your cue."

Peter remained where he was, while Lauren disappeared into the wings and moments later climbed the two steps of the balcony platform. She held on to the railing as Peter said his opening line, paused for a moment, and then continued. He did not refer to the script in his left hand but rather recited the well-known words:

"But soft, what light through yonder window breaks?
It is the east and Juliet is the sun!
Arise fair sun and kill the envious moon
Who is already sick and pale with grief
That thou her maid art far more fair than she."

He stopped and held up the script. "Simon, I think I'd like to try it off book, but with a prompt available. Can we do it that way?"

"Sure," said Simon, approaching the stage. "That's what I like to hear. We're making progress!" He reached up, took the script from Peter, and handed it to Aaron. "I don't have a copy of the prompt book here, but you can manage with this."

He gestured in the direction of the prompt's seat, a small table with a tiny, bright task light set up behind the curtain closest to the audience. Here, as the play gradually got up on its legs and then into the actual performances, the prompter followed the play's dialogue and action line by line, ready to assist an actor who forgot where he was supposed to stand or what he was supposed to say, hopefully all without the audience hearing.

Simon touched Aaron lightly on the arm. "Before you get up there, I'm desperate for a bottle of water. Can you get me one from the canteen? A cold one. Just run over and tell her it's for me and I'll come by and pay for it later. But make it fast. I don't want to call a full break until we've finished this scene."

As Aaron sped off, Simon addressed the actors. "Those on stage hold your positions. Those of you in the audience, stay where you are. We'll be starting again in a couple of minutes, as soon as Aaron gets back. When we've finished this scene, we'll take a twenty-minute break. I'm sure you can all hang on until then."

Peter sat on the edge of the stage facing the audience, his legs dangling, talking quietly with his new boyfriend, the actor playing Mercutio. Simon paced back and forth across the apron area between the stage and front row of seats, hunched over his phone. He punched the keys for a few minutes and then dropped the phone into his shirt pocket and looked toward the door beside the stage.

Several minutes later, an out-of-breath Aaron thrust a bottle of cold water, dripping with condensation, into Simon's hand.

"About time! What took you so long? It doesn't take ten minutes to get a bottle of water." As Aaron started to reply, Simon interrupted him. "Never mind. I don't want to waste any more time. Come on, let's get going." Aaron clattered up the stairs, slipped behind the curtain, and took his seat at the prompt desk.

"So, Peter, just repeat the last line starting, 'That thou her maid,' and take it from there." Peter, as Romeo, raised his arm in a sweeping, all-encompassing kind of gesture and turned to address his Juliet.

Lauren was not there. Peter turned and looked out to the audience and then walked to the edge of the stage and bent down to speak to the director in his front-row seat.

"Simon . . ."

"Yes, Peter?" There was just the smallest hint of annoyance in his voice, while the unspoken "What is it now?" hung in the air.

"Simon, Lauren's not here." He gestured at the empty stage behind him. "She didn't say anything to me about going somewhere, and I didn't see her leave." He peered at his castmates seated in the audience. "I don't see her out there, either."

As the short break stretched out, restless cast members scattered throughout the theater stirred in their seats, and two women, seated together near the back, moved to the front, sliding in to sit beside a friend in the third row. A ripple of whispers spread out from them.

"Peter, check the wings and backstage area," Simon said.

The actor walked upstage to the balcony and, seeing a splash of turquoise, turned and called out, "I was wrong. She is here. I think she's collapsed."

Simon sprinted onstage. After taking a quick look at Lauren, he called to Aaron.

"It's too dark. I can't see properly. Have you got a flashlight?"

"No, but I'll bring the lights up."

The other actors were now out of their seats and standing at the edge of the stage. They remained silent but turned anxious, concerned eyes to one another as the full house lights came up to reveal Simon crouched over Lauren's crumpled body. She lay on her side behind the small platform, hidden from the actors' view, eyes open, with her head turned toward the rear of the theater. Her sweater was stained bright red and her arms were limp.

Simon stood up and approached Aaron. "Call the police," he said in a low voice, "and tell them we need an ambulance. I just hope we're not too late." He then turned to Peter, who a few short minutes before had been praising his Juliet but now hovered nearby, speechless and helpless. "Peter, please get off the stage, join the others, and tell them to sit down. Nobody is to leave, and nobody is to come any closer."

Peter did as he was told. A moment later, a stifled scream came from the little group, and the actors clustered around a young woman. One of the older women wrapped her arms around her as another led her to a seat. The only sound was her loud, racking sobs.

A slight movement of curtains made Simon look up to see Charlotte about to step onstage.

"Stay where you are, Charlotte. Don't come any closer," he shouted at her.

"What's the matter? I've just come to collect"—she checked the piece of paper in her hand—"Mercutio for his costume fitting. He's late, and I thought he might be here. Benvolio's due in half an hour. I'm all ready for them."

Simon took a few steps toward her. "Charlotte, don't come any closer," he repeated.

"What is it? Has something happened?"

"It's Lauren. We thought she'd collapsed, and well, she has, but it's bad. Very bad. There's a lot of blood. I think she's been stabbed."

"Stabbed! . . . is she . . . ?"

Simon nodded. "I think so."

"What, here? How can that be?" She peered around the curtain at the actors sitting stiffly in the front row, one with his elbow propped on the armrest, his cheek resting on his closed fist, and his eyes closed. Another was on his phone.

She pointed at them. "Were they out front the whole time? How could she have been stabbed in front of all these people? In front of you?"

"She was at the back of the stage and it was pretty dark. I'm not sure how it happened, to be honest, but Aaron's called for an ambulance and the police, and they should be here any minute. I've asked everyone to remain where they are."

Charlotte took a couple of steps back. "Yes, well, calling the police certainly makes sense. I wonder if I should stay here or go back to the workroom."

"You need to stay here with us. Whoever did this could still be out there. You'll be safer here with us."

"Yes, I suppose you're right." She took another step backward. "Is there anything I can do?"

Simon shook his head. "We just need to stay calm until the police get here to take charge."

The police, Charlotte thought. Ray and Phil? She just couldn't picture them, well-meaning as they were, investigating a murder. As far as she could remember, nothing this bad had happened around here for at least ten years.

About five minutes later, Ray and Phil, followed by a paramedic, entered the backstage area.

"Over here," Simon called from behind the balcony riser where he had remained beside Lauren Richmond. The paramedic stepped onto the stage, crouched over the body, applied his stethoscope, stood up, and shook his head. He returned to Ray, Phil, Charlotte, and Simon, who waited offstage. "No," he said. "I'm sorry, but she's gone."

"Is there someplace we can start to interview everyone?" Ray asked.

"Charlotte's room, perhaps?" said Simon, looking to her for approval. "It's big enough for everyone, and I doubt you'll be doing any fittings this afternoon."

"That'll be fine," she replied and then turned to Ray. "Are you going to . . . ?" She tipped her head in the direction of the stage. "You know. Investigate this?"

"No," said Ray. "We're way out of our depth here. As soon as Aaron called, we notified the BCI. They should be here soon to start processing the scene. We don't have the expertise or equipment for that. In the meantime, the best thing we can do is keep everyone away so we don't contaminate the scene any further."

"BCI?" asked Simon.

"Bureau of Criminal Investigation, New York State Police. They handle major crime for small towns like ours. They'll do the forensics and investigating, and we'll leave everything to them. Now, what's the best way out of here? We don't want anyone traipsing across the stage."

"Aaron will show you," said Charlotte. "There's an exit at the back of the theater that leads to the hotel lobby."

Charlotte hurried back to her workroom, and a few minutes later, the actors, led by Aaron and accompanied by Ray, trooped in. Phil remained in the theater to secure the scene.

"Coffee, hot and strong, I think, Aaron," she said. "Ask for it in a large carafe, not individual cups. And when you've done that, you'd better let your uncle know what's happened."

"There's something else," said Ray. "The BCI will be here soon, and they're going to need an incident room.

Is there a private and secure space they can use? They'll want a room they can lock."

"Well, that's up to Harvey, of course, but perhaps the rehearsal room could be available to them. Simon seems to be holding all his rehearsals onstage. Aaron, can you sort that out with your uncle when you're talking to him?"

"Is there anything else you need me to do?" Aaron asked.

"No," said Charlotte. "That's all I can think of right now. Just bring the coffee, quick as you can, then go see your uncle."

"There's something else we can do to get ready for the BCI," said Ray. "We can eliminate everybody who was in full view of everyone during the time Lauren was last seen and when her body was found."

"Simon's the best one to tell you that." She looked at the little group of actors, clustered together near the wall that contained the bolts of fabric. "I thought Simon came in with the actors, but I guess not. I wonder where he . . ."

The door opened and Simon entered, took in what was happening, and joined Charlotte and Ray.

"Simon, I wonder if you could tell me who was in the theater at the time of the incident, and where they were. We want to eliminate everyone we can," said Ray.

"Sure. Well, there's me, of course. I was down in front. Oh! I sent some texts. You can check my phone, if you want. Then there's Peter, who was rehearsing Romeo. He was on the stage, sitting with his back to Lauren. He was talking to Brent, who's playing Mercutio. I hear they've become, er, close. They were with each other the whole time."

He paused. Ray looked up from his notebook. "There weren't that many there, actually," Simon continued. "The only actors present were the ones involved in the scene we were rehearsing and one or two others." He named the young male actor playing Benvolio, the middle-aged woman playing the nurse, and the middle-aged man playing Friar Lawrence, who appeared in scene 3.

"I can vouch for several more," said Charlotte. "The members of the Capulet household all came at the same time for their fittings, so if one costume didn't suit someone, we could try it immediately on someone else. There were six of them. They didn't require much. They just wear generic costumes. Breeches, shirts, big dresses, and such."

"And their fitting was at the same time as the rehearsal was going on?"

Simon and Charlotte exchanged a quick confirming glance. "Yes," said Charlotte.

Ray turned his attention to Simon. "I'd like to see those texts you sent. The time stamp will tell us exactly what time you called the break." Simon showed him his phone, and Ray noted the time on his notepad. "So ten twenty a.m."

He turned to Charlotte. "And you were doing the fittings at that time? Ten twenty?"

She nodded. "The names are in the day book, and all the actors who were scheduled kept their appointments. They arrived on time, and nobody left early. Actors tend to like costume fittings, even watching someone else trying on a costume. Their parts start to come alive, and the whole theater illusion begins to take shape and come together for them."

"That's right," agreed Simon, as he bestowed a warm smile on her.

Ray frowned and cleared his throat.

"So some of the actors were with Charlotte at the costume fitting, and some were at the rehearsal."

"That's right," said Simon again.

"So does this account for everybody?"

"Not quite," said Simon. "One or two weren't needed for this rehearsal and weren't at the costume fitting, either."

Ray sighed. "It's always complicated, isn't it? Okay. Simon, if you could give me their names, please, I'll pass them on to the BCI team. They'll want to interview everyone we can't exclude. Now, I'm going to have a word with these witnesses, one by one."

Charlotte and Simon watched Ray move to the other side of the room. Simon looked at his water bottle, then

Charlotte. "There's something I didn't mention to the police officer," he said softly.

Charlotte gave him a sharp look. "What's that?"

"When it happened, Aaron wasn't in full sight of everyone. I'd sent him out to get me a bottle of water, and it seemed to take him longer than I thought it should have. And when he got back, he was out of breath."

Chapter 15

Simon looked around Charlotte's wardrobe room. "Where is he now, by the way?" he asked her.

"Who?"

"Aaron."

"He's gone to organize coffee for everyone and then tell his uncle what happened and arrange an interview room for the police," said Charlotte. "Why?"

"I passed him in the hall. Head down, back arched. Looked, well, bothered."

"Of course he's bothered! Aren't we all? Someone was just stabbed to death, and the killer is very likely amongst us."

"Yes, Charlotte, I'm aware of that. I'm sorry. That didn't come out quite right. Let's just say he looked a little more bothered than the rest of them." He gestured at the actors talking to Ray. "They look dazed and confused, understandably, but Aaron looked more than that. He looked troubled. Scared, even."

"You don't think he had anything to do with this, do you?" She glared at him. He raised an eyebrow and shrugged. "You do!"

"Well, in my line of work, we specialize in body language, and frankly, what I saw of him didn't look good."

"Well, I hope the police don't agree with you. I'm sure there's a simple explanation for his whereabouts at the time."

"Do you think I should mention it to the police?"

Charlotte folded her arms and thought for a moment.

"Yes, I think you should. In the end, everything's bound to come out, isn't it? What's that E. M. Forster line from *A Passage to India*? Something like, 'You can do what you like but the outcome will be just the same'? I loved the way Alec Guinness said that in the movie."

"Yes, you might be right. I don't want to get Aaron in trouble, but at the same time, if I don't mention it and the police find out, they might wonder why I didn't say something."

He took a sip of water. "I hope Aaron gets here soon with that coffee." He glanced at Ray, who was closing his notebook. "It's none of my business, but I couldn't help wondering. Is there something between you and the police officer? He seemed a little, I don't know, edgy, just then. A little bit possessive, maybe?"

Charlotte did not reply.

"Oh, dear. Sorry. Did I cross a line there?"

"It's all right." But the hard line of her shoulders, slight frown, and averted eyes told him the question was very much not all right.

While he was thinking of what to say next, trying to find the right words to turn the situation around, Aaron arrived, pushing a small cart laden with coffee and doughnuts. The actors surged toward it, but a moment later, the arrival of Harvey Jacobs silenced everyone. He looked around the room as though seeing it for the first time. He chose a spot in front of the cutting table and, with his hands behind his back, leaned against it.

"If I could just ask for your attention for a few minutes," he began. "My nephew here," he nodded in Aaron's direction, "has just informed me about this terrible tragedy. I understand the police are here, and I expect every one of you will give them your full cooperation. They will get to the bottom of this. In the meantime, I want to reassure you that you are in no danger."

"And how does he know that?" Simon muttered.

"He's saying it to provide reassurance and let everyone know he's in control," Charlotte whispered. "It's his idea of what a leader is supposed to do."

Harvey invited the cast members to help themselves to coffee, as Ray joined Simon and Charlotte to tell them he was leaving to await the arrival of the state police.

*

The sound of several vehicles approaching the hotel got Brian Prentice's attention. Curious, he got up from the table in the bungalow where he and his wife had been enjoying a late-morning cup of coffee and pulled back the curtain, revealing a dark blue car emblazoned with "New York State Trooper" on the side. It was followed by another police car and then two vans.

"Something must have happened in the hotel," he said to his wife.

She looked up from her newspaper and took a sip of coffee. "Well, that'll make a change."

"No, really, there's police cars everywhere. Oh, and now here comes an ambulance." He watched its progress and then let out a little gasp. "Oh, dear. That's not a good sign."

"Mmm?" said his wife.

"I said that's not a good sign. An ambulance has arrived but it's not got its lights flashing or siren switched on. That leads me to think somebody is already past helping."

"Oh," said Lady Deborah. "I wonder who." She thought for a moment. "Harvey, perhaps? He's been looking a little peaky lately, I thought. And all that extra weight isn't helping. It'll be the stress of running his non-profit establishment, I shouldn't wonder."

"Really, Deborah. Must you?" Brian pulled his jacket off a hook by the door and slid his arms down the sleeves.

"But if it is Harvey, I wonder if my contract would still be valid."

"Well, you'd best go and find out, hadn't you?" She turned her newspaper to the arts section. "I wonder what's playing on Broadway. Maybe we could treat ourselves to a little outing and see a real play. You'd like that, wouldn't you, Brian? Make a nice night out for you."

Brian groaned and let the screen door slam behind him. Stuffing his hands into the pockets of his jacket and hunching against the wind, he made his way to the hotel. The sounds of men's voices somewhere off to his left drew him to the loading zone behind the stage, so he headed in that direction. At the entrance to the backstage area, Phil Davenport, who had been protecting the crime scene, held up his hand.

"Sorry, sir, you can't go in there."

"What's going on? I saw the police cars and ambulance and want to find out what's happening. Is somebody hurt?"

"And you are, sir?"

"I'm Brian Prentice. I'm the lead actor here."

"Well, in that case, you might want to join the others. They're in the costume department, so I'm told. Back down the hall the way you came, past the rear entrance, and carry on. On your right. I'm not allowed to give out any information, but I'm sure your colleagues will be more than happy to fill you in."

Brian turned on his heel and marched down the hall. As he reached the back door to the hotel, he spotted a tall man carrying a notebook and wearing a fedora and an imitation Burberry raincoat just inside the entrance. The man hesitated, as if unsure which way to go.

"There's no point going down that way," said Brian, gesturing toward the stage area. "I've just come from there. I spoke to a police officer, and no one is being admitted. Something's happened but I don't know what." He held out his hand. "Brian Prentice."

"Sir Brian!" said the man, clasping Brian's hand in a limp, damp shake. "Delighted! Fletcher Macmillan, arts reporter."

Brian did not bother to correct him. *Sir Brian!* Oh, how he liked the sound of that. If the fools who made those decisions had had their wits about them, he would have been knighted years ago. And why not him? It made more sense than some of the other fellows who'd had the honor of kneeling on the knighting stool whilst the Queen or Prince Charles tapped them on their shoulders with the ceremonial sword, rewarding them "for services to the arts" and bestowing on them not just a fancy title but all kinds of benefits as well, although Brian wasn't quite sure what the additional benefits were. Anyway, men younger than he who hadn't accomplished nearly as much, like rock and roll musicians, had had their day at Buckingham Palace, and he had not. Oh, yes, he could name names.

"Yes, there's definitely something going on," said Fletcher, returning Brian to the present. "We heard something on the police scanner."

"I've just spoken to the police officer," Brian repeated, "but he was unable or unwilling to provide me with information. He suggested I join the others in the costume department, so I was going down there."

"Well, now there's a coincidence!" said Fletcher. "I was just headed there myself, so if you wouldn't mind leading the way? I assume you do know the way."

"Down here. And perhaps you could enlighten me as we go. It's serious, I imagine, this situation."

"You mean you don't know?" said Fletcher.

"No. I've been learning lines in my bungalow all morning. Haven't been near the place."

"Our editor heard on the police radio that someone had been injured here. They weren't too specific, but they never are over the radio." And then he added, with no apparent sense of irony, "They never know who might be listening, so they keep everything on the down low." As the two men approached the door to the wardrobe room, he continued. "I did try the front entrance, but couldn't raise anyone, so thought I'd try my luck back here."

Brian opened the door. Fletcher, peering over his shoulder at the various cast members, and realizing he was in a target-rich environment, remarked, "This seems to be where it's all happening, for sure."

Two or three actors were chatting quietly in the subdued atmosphere. Immediately as Fletcher and Brian entered, anxious, expectant eyes turned in their direction and the room fell silent.

"What's going on?" asked Brian in his sonorous voice.

On the other side of the room, Simon raised an eyebrow, and Charlotte, seeing Brian, fingered the collar of her shirt and adjusted the sleeves of her cardigan.

"He's your actor, Simon," she said. "You'd better deal with him." As Simon took his first steps toward Brian, she scurried past the actors into the adjoining room where the costumes were stored. She leaned against the wall and waited for her embarrassed heart to stop pounding.

Simon strode over to the pair and, after eyeing Fletcher up and down, addressed him. "Would you mind? I'd like a private word with Brian." Fletcher shrugged and stepped away but remained within earshot.

"It's very bad news, I'm afraid, Brian," said Simon in a soft voice. "It's Lauren. She was injured while we were rehearsing, and I'm sorry to have to tell you this, but she's dead."

Brian raised his hands to his face and covered his mouth. "Dead," he breathed. "Oh, dear God, what happened? Was it an accident? Did she fall?"

"No, Brian, it wasn't an accident. It looks like she was stabbed. The police are here, and they've opened a full-scale homicide investigation."

"Homicide," boomed Brian in a voice that filled the room. "Oh, our beautiful girl murdered. How could this have happened? Who has done this terrible deed?"

"We don't know yet, but I'm sure the police will find the person responsible."

"Miscreant! Assassin!" shouted Brian, raising a fist.

"Listen, you've got to calm down, Brian," said Simon, placing what was meant to be a reassuring hand on Brian's arm. "Get a hold of yourself. We don't want to upset the young ones."

"No, I suppose not," agreed Brian, lowering his arm. The young ones smirked at one another, unsure exactly what they'd just seen, but having enjoyed it hugely.

"Have you ever seen such an over-the-top reaction?" giggled one.

"Never. It was fascinating. I couldn't take my eyes off him. It was like old-school grand theater. Wish I'd caught it on my phone."

"He certainly seemed shocked and surprised, didn't he?"

"Did he? Or was that just a Shakespearean actor's version of shock and surprise?"

"Who's that guy with you, as if I couldn't guess?" Simon asked Brian.

"Said he was an arts reporter."

Simon now turned his attention to Fletcher Macmillan, who had been scribbling furiously. "I'm sorry, Mr. . . ."

"Macmillan. Fletcher Macmillan. I'm the arts reporter with the *Hudson Valley Echo*. You're Simon Dyer, the director, aren't you? Recognized you from the photographs. I wonder if you'd be kind enough to give me a few minutes of your time. This is going to be big news around here, I can tell you."

"It's not up to me to say anything to the press," said Simon. "It's the hotel owner and police you need to speak to, and I'm sorry, but I'm going to have to ask you leave. This area is for the company."

He took Macmillan by the arm and was preparing to escort him out when the door opened and Harvey Jacobs reentered.

"This could be your lucky day," hissed Simon to Macmillan.

"I thought I'd just check back in," Harvey Jacobs lowered his voice and spoke directly to Simon, "to see if there've been any developments."

Simon shook his head. "No, Harvey. Nothing new. But there's someone here who wants to ask you a few questions." He introduced Fletcher Macmillan, who handed Jacobs his card.

"Let's go to my office," said Harvey, putting a friendly arm around Fletcher's shoulder and steering him toward the door. "We can talk there. I'll tell you what I know, which isn't very much. You'll get more information from the police, I'm sure. You've given us some wonderful reviews in the past, and you really must come see what we're putting on this season. We have a splendid run planned with top-notch performers." His voice trailed off as the two disappeared down the hall and Simon closed the door behind them.

"The police have asked those who were in the theater this morning to wait here, Brian," Simon said. "As that doesn't include you, it might be best if you left now, before the state police arrive to begin the investigation."

Brian mulled that over for a moment, and then, after taking a long, close look around the room, left.

As soon as the door closed behind him, Simon made his way past the actors into the costume storage area. "It's okay. He's gone. You can come out now. I don't think he saw you."

Charlotte emerged from behind a costume rack. "I'm sorry. I just couldn't face him right now. Not today. I've managed to avoid him so far, and I know I'll have to deal with him, but just not yet. I suppose you think me very cowardly."

"Feel like telling me?"

"It was a long time ago. We were . . ."

"Involved?"

"Yes, involved. And then he dumped me, saying he was going to marry Lady Deborah. I was so naïve. So stupid. I didn't even know he was seeing someone else." She glanced at him. "I was devastated. And felt like such a fool. An idiot. Still do, come to that."

"He's the fool, if you ask me. Giving you up for a joy-less life with that . . . well, never mind. This isn't the right time. Let's go out and see how the kids are holding up."

Aaron had taken it upon himself to use the time to fit Peter Simmonds with his Romeo costume while his friend who played the part of Mercutio sat close by. The others had scattered around the room. One or two, heads down and focused on their phones, were oblivious to what was going on around them, while two others were running lines.

"Hey, Simon, how much longer do we have to hang around here?" an actor called out. "We're getting hungry."

"Good question," said Charlotte. "Let's find out."

She picked up her phone and pressed Ray's number. When he answered, she listened for a moment and then ended the call.

"He said the state officers are on their way to inter-view them. Should be here soon. So while they're wait-ing, why don't you and I get them some sandwiches and drinks from the canteen," Charlotte said to Simon. "It'll help to pass the time, if nothing else. But they mustn't eat anywhere near my costumes or fabrics. That's the rule."

"Good idea," said Simon. "Let's do it."

Just as they entered the main hallway, Simon smiled down at her at the same instant as she lifted her face to him to say something. At that moment, unknown to them, Ray turned the corner in the corridor a few feet behind them. Seeing them, he frowned.

They paused as Charlotte said something to Simon that he didn't quite catch. He lowered his head toward her in a natural listening gesture and touched her arm. The sun slanting in from high windows bathed them in a soft, warm light.

Ray's frown turned into a dark scowl as Simon and Charlotte disappeared together into the canteen. He turned around when Phil placed a hand on his shoulder.

"Hey, boss."

"Yeah, Phil, what is it?"

"The state boys have just arrived."

"Okay, thanks for letting me know."

"Everything all right? This getting to you? You sound a little, I don't know, peeved."

Ray squared his shoulders and gave Phil what he hoped was a reassuring, steady look.

"No, I'm fine. Let's go open the door for the Albany team."

But the image of Charlotte smiling at that director stayed with him, and he didn't like the way it made him feel. Not one bit.

*

Fletcher Macmillan shook Harvey Jacobs's hand and left his office. He could hardly believe his luck. This could be the big break he'd been waiting for. His interview with Lauren Richmond at the hospital was the last one she'd given, and now she'd gone and got herself murdered! And

Harvey Jacobs had opened up like he couldn't believe. If Fletcher played his cards right, this story could be career changing. He'd call the *New York Times* right away, and then head back to the newsroom and start writing.

But first, a late lunch. He'd had nothing since breakfast and was starving. He got in his car and drove into town. At the diner, he ordered a BLT and a chocolate milkshake. While he waited for it, he flipped through his notebook, reviewed his notes, and then called his contact at the *New York Times*. He explained what had happened in Walkers Ridge, how he'd got interviews with the victim and the hotel owner. This story had everything going for it! A young, beautiful victim, stabbed just as she teetered on the brink of stardom. He fingered the menu while he waited for a response, and then a slow smile spread across his face as he made a fist and pulled it toward his body.

"I'm on it," he said before pressing the red "end call" button. When the waitress appeared with his food, he told her to wrap it up and that he'd take it with him. Who had time for lunch when the *New York Times* was waiting for him, Fletcher Macmillan, its newest stringer from the Hudson Valley, to file his story?

Chapter 16

Simon Dyer was exhausted; he couldn't remember the last time he'd felt so drained. All that waiting around, trying to keep the actors' spirits up. And then answering the police officers' endless questions. They were professional, he'd give them that. But even when you'd done nothing wrong, being interviewed by a trained police officer was still intimidating, even though he didn't think they suspected him. How could they? He'd been front of house, not even on the stage, in full view of everybody the whole time. Still, they'd taken his fingerprints, along with everyone else's, so they could "eliminate you from our inquiry." But his record was bound to show up when the prints were matched, and they might take a second look at him. When they'd finished with him this afternoon, they'd advised him that they might want to speak to him again.

One thing about the police interview bothered him, though. They'd asked if anyone was out of his sight and unaccounted for during the break when Lauren was presumed to have been murdered. Did anyone leave the room?

He'd told them Aaron had gone off on an errand and was gone a little longer than he, Simon, would have expected. He'd hesitated over his response. Not because he felt any particular loyalty to Aaron—he barely knew the kid—he just wasn't comfortable giving up too much information. But he had to say something. He'd discussed what to do with Charlotte and agreed with her that if the police found out about it later, as they probably would, they'd wonder why he hadn't mentioned it. Inwardly, he shrugged. Maybe it wouldn't matter. Either it was important or it wasn't. If Aaron hadn't done anything wrong, then he had nothing to worry about.

He trudged across the parking lot at the rear of the hotel, his footsteps crunching on the gravel. The state troopers' cars and van were gone; just one car bearing the livery of the local police department remained. A pale moon hung in the darkening sky, occasionally obscured by drifting clouds. He paused for a moment to gaze up. Without the light pollution of an urban environment, the night sky seemed deeper and darker here, and the stars showcased so much brighter, like diamonds against a black velvet backdrop. At another time, another place in his life, he might have enjoyed the lightscape above him.

But not here and not now. He knew from his job interview with Harvey Jacobs that this place was isolated, but he hadn't realized how the isolation would impact him. It wasn't so bad in the daytime when he was busy and people were about, and it was bound to improve when the season got going, but he was finding the evenings long and lonely.

He set off again. A light coming from Charlotte's bungalow, diffused behind a closed curtain, gave off a warm, inviting look. He hesitated for a moment, wanting to knock on her door under some vague pretext or other that might get him invited in, but he couldn't come up with anything that didn't sound ridiculously stupid, never mind even remotely plausible. She'd lived and worked here at the Jacobs Grand Hotel a long time, someone had told him. He wondered what had brought her here and why she'd stayed so long. Did she have a circle of close friends in town? Or did she keep to herself and that's the way she liked it? He remembered the feeling of jealousy he'd picked up from the police officer and wondered again what they meant to each other.

He smiled to himself. In a way, he and the police officer had more in common than might at first be apparent. As a theater director, he too dealt in motivation fueled by the complete range of human emotions, some exposed, some carefully hidden. Truth, lies, regret, greed, jealousy, deception, yearning, honesty, and redemption drove the stories he worked so hard to bring to life. Shakespeare was all about the examined life.

He hadn't always been a Shakespeare director, nor had he always lived on the East Coast. Back in Colorado, he'd started out in community theater, working his way into bigger and more professional productions until he found himself in New York. Off Broadway, then on. Big stars, big budgets, big dreams, big risks, big rewards. And then came the cocaine years—endless days and nights of snow blindness, bringing people he didn't want into his life. But they came with the territory and took away what was left of his ambition. And finally came the night when his life, or what was left of it, crashed and burned.

He put the key in the lock and opened the door to his bungalow. It was the same size as Charlotte's, but where she had made hers a home, his was a temporary place with all the damp, musty charm of a roadside cabin with cheap pine paneling in the off season. Except for his clothes, a few books, and a laptop, there were no personal items. No photos sat on a side table, no artwork graced a wall.

He hung up his coat, switched on the electric heater to try to take some of the dampness away, and sat down. He'd eaten a solitary dinner in the canteen, so there was not even the diversion of having to prepare a meal. He hated television and, except for the occasional documentary or news program, rarely watched it. He thought for a moment and then pulled out the business card he'd picked up on Charlotte's desk that afternoon. He looked at his house phone and then stretched out on the sofa.

Not tonight, but one night, and soon, he would call her. A whole summer stretched in front of him, and he should make the most of it. It was time he stopped punishing himself and got on with his life. As the saying goes, life is for the living.

Which reminded him. He'd have to find an actress to replace Lauren. That shouldn't be too hard. Word that a part was up for grabs even in a place like this spread like wildfire through the New York agents' offices. He'd place a call in the morning and get that ball rolling. He checked his watch. Not too late for a cup of coffee, so he went to the kitchen and switched on the kettle. While he waited for it to boil, he glanced out the window at the lights in Charlotte's bungalow and wondered what she was doing.

*

"Are you hungry?" Ray asked. "If you are, we could go into town and get something to eat. It's not that late."

Charlotte shook her head. "No, I couldn't eat a thing. How about you? There's some leftover chicken; I could make you a sandwich."

"That would be nice. And a cup of coffee to go with it would really hit the spot."

Ray studied her as she pulled a plastic container out of the fridge and set it on the counter.

"I wish I could talk to you about this case," he said, "but I'm not supposed to. It's operational. Sharing information with someone, even someone like you that I trust, could jeopardize the investigation. Or worse. Saw a watertight case thrown out of court once because a detective told his wife something that turned out to be important, and she shared it with her bridge club. And one of the bridge-club ladies shared it with her brother-in-law, who just happened to be the defense attorney. The judge had no choice but to declare a mistrial." He reached for the cup of coffee Charlotte held out to him. "True story."

Charlotte washed her hands, dried them on a clean towel, and began slicing a chicken breast. "Did I ask you about the case? Of course you can't tell me anything," she said. "I wouldn't expect you to."

"What do you know about this Simon character?" Ray asked.

"Not much. He's only been here a few weeks. Seems competent enough as a director. The actors respect him. Overheard him warning Brian Prentice about his drinking. Let me see. When was that? Seems like days, weeks ago. Anyway, he told Brian he had to knock the drinking on its head because it's putting his career in jeopardy and this is probably his last chance to save what's left of it."

"Well, he should know about last chances," said Ray.

"Who should?"

"Well, isn't this Dyer's last chance?"

"I don't know. Is it?"

Ray did not reply. Charlotte finished assembling the sandwich, cut it in half, and handed the plate to Ray. "Do you want to eat at the table or on the couch?"

"How about on the couch? The evening news is about to start. I want to see if there's anything about our murder."

Charlotte switched on the television, and an image of Lauren filled the screen behind the newsreader. She put her arm around Rupert, who always sat on the couch with her.

"I guess her family's been notified," Ray remarked, "or they wouldn't be showing her photo like that. At least, I'd hope not."

The newscaster's voice filled the room. "We begin our news coverage tonight with the murder of an up-and-coming actress at a Catskills resort. Lauren Richmond, twenty-three, was stabbed to death this morning during a rehearsal of *Romeo and Juliet* at Jacobs Grand Hotel. Details are still sketchy, but we hope to bring you more by the end of the broadcast." The newsreader continued with the day's top stories and then introduced the weather specialist.

"I didn't know they did Shakespeare in the Catskills," the meteorologist remarked in the folksy bit of banter that the presenters always engaged in. "Well, they can prepare for rain and dropping temperatures. We've got some stormy weather coming in over the next forty-eight hours. I'll tell you all about it after the break."

Ray took a deep breath. "Well, the news is out there now. There could be television crews here tomorrow."

"Thanks for the warning." Charlotte picked up her telephone and dialed Harvey's extension. When Aaron picked up, she told him to tell his uncle to prepare for media that could be arriving in the morning. He thanked her, and she returned to Ray.

"That was Aaron."

"So I gathered. He's a person of interest to the investigation."

"Why?"

"Because according to one witness, he was out of sight during the time the murder was committed. That makes the Albany boys very curious."

"You don't think that he had anything to do with it, do you?"

"Well why not? Apparently he had the opportunity, and you told me yourself he had a motive."

"What motive?"

"She bullied his cousin to death. He must have hated her."

"Well, yes, but that doesn't make him a killer."

"No, of course it doesn't. But the detectives will be taking a pretty close look at him."

Charlotte gave him a sharp look. "And why is that, exactly?"

"Because there's no one else in the frame at this point. So far, everyone else is accounted for."

"Was Aaron interviewed today?" she asked.

"Yes, briefly. Why?"

She sat back. "I don't think he did it," she said firmly.

"Look, Charlotte, people always say that about some-one they know when there's been a murder. Mind you, they're usually talking about a family member, but some-times it's a neighbor."

"Is he going to be arrested?"

"Not yet. The detectives have still got a case to build."

"I thought you weren't supposed to discuss the case with me."

"I'm not. You didn't hear any of this from me. This conversation never took place."

She smiled. "Why are you telling me all this?"

"All what?"

*

In his apartment in the hotel, Harvey Jacobs checked the company e-mail. Since the news broadcast, ten reserva-tions had been booked.

"Aaron," he called to his nephew. "Do you know anybody who can update the website? We need to get our summer program up there right away. In fact, we're going to be so busy over the next few days, I'm going to call Nancy and see if she'll come back to work." Aaron looked up from the game he was playing on his iPad. He was a little startled by the broad smile on his uncle's face.

"This is the summer we turn the corner, my boy," he said. "If I'd known murder could be so good for business, I'd have . . ." He caught himself and let out a low little chuckle.

"Well, never mind. I wonder how much it would cost to give the lobby a bit of a makeover. Freshen things up. Smarten up the place. It's looking a little tired, don't you think?"

Chapter 17

As the meteorologist had predicted on the evening news, the next morning did indeed bring lower temperatures. In fact, it was one of those cold days that remind those who live in northern climates that winter always rallies for one last blast. Just when you think it's safe to put away your boots and heavy coat, you find yourself scurrying to the closet for the wooly things you hoped you wouldn't need again until fall.

Charlotte awoke to hard, driving rain pelting against her bedroom window. On days like this, she wished she could give the dog walking a miss, and although she pulled the blankets more tightly around her, there was no escaping it. Time to get up.

She took a croissant from the freezer and left it on the counter to thaw while she dressed warmly, put Rupert on his leash, and headed outside. Twenty minutes later—both of them wet, cold, and miserable—they entered the bungalow. While Rupert ate his breakfast, Charlotte had her morning shower. And then, sipping a warming mug of coffee and munching the croissant slathered with strawberry jam, she watched the morning news. The lead story was the weather, with images of discarded umbrellas, their ribs broken from having been blown inside out once too often, tossed into Wall Street trash bins. In times of severe weather like this, her walk to work seemed pretty good.

She mulled over last night's conversation with Ray and his suggestion that the police thought Aaron was involved. She was certain he wasn't. She thought Simon had said something that excluded Aaron but couldn't for the life of her remember what it was. *Oh well,* she told herself. *Leave it alone and it'll come to you.*

She set her dishes in the sink, got dressed, and rooted around in her closet for an umbrella. Since she was British, everyone assumed she was used to cold, rainy days (which she was), but she didn't like them nearly as much as everyone seemed to think she should. Rain and wind assaulted her as soon as she closed the door, and after slogging through puddles in her high rubber boots, she was relieved to reach the hotel. She shook the rain off her umbrella and opened the door to find Aaron just inside.

"Morning, Aaron. What are you doing here? Are you waiting for me?"

"Yeah."

"Any particular reason?"

"Yeah, sort of. We've got a full day of costume fittings, and since it's going to be so busy, I wanted to make sure I had a chance to talk to you before the actors arrive."

"Right. Let's stop off in the canteen and treat ourselves to some coffee. Then we'll talk."

Once they had their mugs of coffee, Charlotte handed hers to Aaron while she unlocked the door to her costume department. As soon as the door was open, he slipped past her with the coffees and set them down on her desk. She opened her umbrella and propped it up in the hall to dry and then followed him in.

"Now then, young sir. We're pressed for time to get set up, so let's get right to it," she said to Aaron. "What's bothering you?"

"It's about my uncle."

She took a sip of coffee, waited, and then raised an eyebrow.

"Aaron. Just tell me."

"After you called last night, he asked if I could find someone to update the website."

"Good. Nothing wrong with that. It hasn't been updated since last year. It needs it."

"He said bookings were starting to come in because of the publicity around the murder. And then he said something like, 'If I'd known murder would be this good for business, I would have . . .' And then he stopped short and talked about redecorating the lobby."

"Which, God knows, it could use. Anyway, you were thinking he was going to say something like . . . ?"

"Well, it seemed to me he was going to say something like, 'I would have done it years ago.'"

"Well, even if that's what he was going to say, that's not a confession! That's the same as saying something like, 'I could have killed her,' when you're mad at someone. It doesn't mean anything."

Aaron frowned and said nothing.

"Surely you don't think your uncle killed Lauren?" When Aaron didn't reply, she gently touched his arm. "Do you?"

"Well, I've been telling him for a long time that he needs a gimmick. He needs to do something different to bring in more customers. Guests. Theatergoers. Whatever you want to call them. Anyway, you should have seen his face when I told him that Leah—Lauren—was the girl who'd bullied my cousin to death. When she died, my aunt died, too, in a way. She was never the same. The light and the life went out of her, that's how my mother described it. And my aunt and my uncle were very close. He always used to say he wished he could share her pain, to lighten her load. And now, maybe he found a way to do something."

"I hope not. But I can see why you'd be worried. Listen, I wouldn't mention this to the police, if I were you. Let them investigate and go where the evidence leads them. But you don't want to put any daft ideas in their heads."

They've already got enough ideas about you, she thought. And then something else occurred to her. What if Aaron was making all this up to throw suspicion on someone else and away from himself?

She gave him a shrewd look and then checked her watch. The first actors would be here any moment for their fittings, and time was going to be tight. They had to stick to the schedule.

"We've got to get set up for the fittings now," she said. "But we'll continue this chat, if you like. Maybe over lunch.

"Now here's what I want you to do. To save a lot of running back and forth, take the morning fitting schedule into the costume storage room, get an empty clothes rack, and pull the costumes we'll need and wheel 'em out. Then we'll open the door and bring in the actors and get on with it."

*

The morning flew by. They measured, adjusted, cajoled, explained, and helped actors in and out of costumes.

"Aaron here will give you a hand with that. We don't have the luxury of a dresser, unless, of course, you count Aaron."

They listened to complaints: "I'm a size twelve."

"Well, maybe you used to be a size twelve, but according to this tape measure, you're a size sixteen. Try this costume on, and if it's too big, we'll take it in or find you something else."

And because several of the actors were fresh out of drama school and their only experience was college productions, Charlotte answered questions: "I really want to get into the part. What kind of underwear should I wear?"

"Well, if you want to be true to the Elizabethans, then you'd wear a smock, stockings, and a corset that hadn't been washed for ages. But do us all a favor, love. Your basic Fruit of the Looms will work just fine."

And then it was lunchtime. When the last actor had left, Charlotte hung up the last pair of puffy shorts known as trunks and sighed.

"Well, there's your afternoon's work cut out for you. You'll have to get started on the adjustments. And when you've done that, put one of these tags on each garment"—she held up a green tag to slip over the hanger—"so we'll know it's done. Then we have to get everyone back in here to try on the costumes again to make sure the alterations are right. They have to look good and be comfortable so the actor can walk easily in them and turn in all directions." Aaron lifted his tape measure off his neck, rolled it up, and placed in on the desk. "In most small, regional theaters like ours, costumes only come in two sizes: too big or too small. But we can do better than that and give our actors that little extra boost of confidence that comes from knowing they look the part and they feel right in their apparel. When the costume doesn't feel like a costume, our work is done."

He did not reply.

"Aaron! I don't think you've heard a word I said. What is it now?"

"I can't stop thinking about my uncle." He looked at her with earnest, pleading eyes. "You know him as well as anyone. Do you think he could have done it?"

"I think anyone, under the right circumstances, is capable of murder. We like to think it's something we couldn't possibly do, but really, until we're tested, how can we know?"

He jumped down off her desk. "I'm not hungry. I think I'll get some air."

"Are you working with Simon this afternoon or coming back here?"

"Simon's gone into the city to meet with a friend of his at one of the drama schools. He needs to find a replacement for . . . her . . . as soon as possible."

"Who have we got booked in this afternoon? We must have seen almost everyone."

"Brian Prentice is the only one booked. We're doing all his costumes for all three of his plays today."

"Are we now?"

"When I set up his costume fitting, he said that's how he wanted it done, so I booked him in by himself and gave him extra time."

Charlotte's throat went a little dry at the mention of his name. This was the encounter she knew was coming but had been absolutely dreading. But now, it seemed that it couldn't be put off any longer.

"Ah, Aaron, I think it would be better if I looked after Brian on my own. For the first, let's say, half hour, anyway."

For the first time that morning, Aaron looked interested.

"Oh? And are you going to tell me why that is?"

"No, Aaron, I'm not. So if Simon isn't here to keep you busy, you should speak to your uncle. I'm sure he'll find something for you to do. Maybe you could do a few sketches on what you think the lobby should look like. Or—what about this? If he wants to smarten the place up, what about designing some new uniforms for the summer staff? Start with the reception desk. You know how important first impressions are. And if he's getting a new lobby, he can't have someone on reception in the same old shabby clothes."

"That's a terrific idea, Charlotte. I'll tell him." As he gathered up his belongings, Charlotte went to the storage cupboard.

"I think I have a brand new sketchbook here just for you. Always start a new project with a new sketchbook."

Aaron looked a little uncomfortable. "That's all right, Charlotte. Thanks just the same, but we don't use sketchbooks anymore. We have apps on our iPads. Well, see you."

Oh, God. I feel about as old as Brian Prentice looks, Charlotte thought.

*

At a few minutes to one, Charlotte opened the door to her costume and wardrobe department and positioned herself just inside it, her hands clasped in front of her. She'd thought about being seated at her desk with her back to the door and then turning around with a casual, "Oh, hello, Brian," when he walked in. But she wasn't sure she could pull it off in a nonchalant, uncaring way.

She hoped to God he wouldn't want to hug her when he arrived. *No*, she reassured herself. *He's British. He hasn't been in the States long enough to pick up that awful habit. So familiar and intrusive, touching someone you've only just met.*

Her hands felt a little clammy, and she ran them down the side of her skirt. And then checked her watch. Five past. A moment later, the sound of footsteps in the hall signaled his arrival. She put on her best professional smile and, hoping her nervousness didn't show, prepared to meet him.

"Hello, Charlotte."

"Oh! Ray! Gosh, what are you doing here?" she stammered. "You surprised me. I wasn't expecting to see you."

"I had a few minutes, so thought I'd drop in and see how you're doing." He frowned slightly. "Who were you expecting?"

"Ah, well, actually, an actor was due at one for a fitting. Brian Prentice, actually." She glanced at the door and cleared her throat.

"You just said 'actually' twice. You seem a little twitchy. Is everything all right?"

"Oh, yes, just fine." She gave herself a silent kick. *What is it about us Brits that no matter how dire things are, if someone asks if everything's all right, it absolutely is? And not only that, we smile when we say it. Why can't we be honest and say, "No, everything is not all right. It's never been worse."* She gave him a weak smile. "Really, Ray, I think it would best if you . . . we could meet up later, perhaps . . ."

A shape loomed in the doorway, immediately followed by Brian's booming voice.

"Well, if it isn't our little Charlotte. I've caught glimpses of you here and there, and I've been so looking forward to seeing you again and catching up on old times." He entered the room and, catching sight of Ray in his blue uniform, held out his hand. "And you must be working on the murder case." He shook his hand. "I'm Brian Prentice. Pleasure to meet you."

Ray looked from one to the other, at Charlotte's drawn, anxious face and Brian's florid, sallow one, with the deep lines of a heavy drinker and smoker. With a last, questioning look at Charlotte, he left, leaving the door open.

Alone with Brian, Charlotte decided to let him speak first.

"Well, Charlotte, it's been a long time."

"Yes, it has. A lot of water under the bridge." She took a step backward. "Now, I've pulled all your costumes here, so we'd best get started." And then, in a moment of blind panic, she realized she didn't want to get too close to him, let alone touch him. The sight of his distended alcoholic belly and sagging skin repulsed her.

She should have made sure that Aaron would be here. She checked her watch in a way that she hoped didn't show. She'd have to get through about twenty minutes. Hopefully Aaron would arrive early. If not, she'd have to find an excuse to ring him.

"Aaron will be here in a few minutes, and he'll take your measurements and do the actual fittings," she said. "My plan was to show you the costumes I've chosen for each play, and you can tell me if you like them, or if you have any special requests, we can try to accommodate them, although we don't have the budget to make new ones for you. Now," she pulled a cloak from the rack, "here's the Montague color. The costumes are designed so the Capulets and Montagues each have their own color."

Brian guffawed. "Teams, as it were."

"Yes, exactly. It helps the audience keep track of who's who. So the Montagues are in the blues. Royal blue, navy blue, dark blues. And the Capulets will be in burgundies, reds . . . those colors." She fingered the end of the tape measure that always hung around her neck.

Brian put his hand on top of the cloak and leaned on it. "You know, Charlotte, you have never been far from my thoughts."

Oh, God, she thought. *Here we go.* Why couldn't he have just been professional?

"Brian, please, I'd rather not talk about it. It was a long time ago, and a lot's happened since then. We aren't the same people."

"Oh, I agree. A lot of water under the bridge, as you said. I thought of contacting you many times but didn't know where you were. I knew you'd stayed behind in America, and I just sort of assumed you were in New York, but I didn't expect you'd be in a place like this."

"You mean the Catskills?"

"Yes."

She decided not to respond. She didn't need to justify her life to him. Over the past few days, she'd realized that she'd given him far too much power over her happiness. She'd spent all those years cherishing the memory of someone who had disappeared long ago. He was now an aging alcoholic, barely able to hold down a last-chance job. He could have been so much, and this is what became of him. Would this have been her life if she'd stayed with him? Looking after this husk of someone who'd shown so much promise and then thrown it all away? And in that moment, as the memories flooded back, she realized she was grateful beyond words to Lady Deborah for sparing her this burden.

"Look, let's be professional about this, shall we, Brian? I've got to show you these clothes, and you need to tell me what you think about them. That's all."

"I made a terrible mistake, you know, Charlotte. I wonder what might have been if only I'd . . ." Brian said, as if he hadn't heard her.

"Well, we'll never know, will we?"

Her face lit up with relief and her knees started to wobble as Aaron walked into the room. "Thought you could use a cup of tea, Charlotte," he said, and then glancing at Brian, he added, "Oh, sorry, I should have remembered you'd be here and brought an extra one. I'll go get one. Won't be a moment."

"No, no. He can have that one," said Charlotte at the same time as Brian said, "That's all right, lad. Never touch the stuff. Thanks just the same."

"Well, Aaron," said Charlotte briskly, not really caring if the relief showed in her voice, "now that you're here, I'm going to leave the rest of the fitting in your more-than-capable hands." With a polite smile at Brian and a sunny, grateful one in Aaron's direction, she left to find Ray.

But what she really wanted to do was go home and have a shower.

Chapter 18

She found Ray leaving the rehearsal room, which the state police had set up as an incident room. She tried to peer around him to get a glimpse at what was going on inside, but he moved slightly to block her view.

"It's operational and filled with confidential material," he said. "Sorry. Not for your eyes."

"Where are you going?"

"They don't need me here anymore, so I'm heading back to the office," he said. "Got a lot of reports to catch up on. And those parking tickets don't give themselves out."

"Oh, I'm glad I caught you, then," she said. "I'll walk out with you."

They strolled in silence to the back door and then entered the parking lot. The rain had just about stopped, and the air smelled fresh and new, lightly laced with the scent of damp earth and wet bark. Large raindrops dripped from the trees onto the sodden ground, washing away the last traces of dirty snow.

"Why don't you ride into town with me, and we'll get a coffee at Bentley's?" Ray suggested.

"Yeah, good idea. I'd like that." She walked around to the passenger side and climbed in. As they drove past the community swimming pool and fitness center, Charlotte made a note to herself that she'd missed too many aquafit classes lately and she should call in and sign up for the spring session.

A few minutes later, Ray parked in front of Bentley's, the café on Main Street once known for its homey comfort meals, like ham and scalloped potatoes, fried chicken and home fries, macaroni and cheese, and old-fashioned pies. Now it was catering to the increasingly sophisticated demands of younger diners with menu items like goat cheese and pear salad or turkey, brie, and green apple on ciabatta bread, with cappuccinos and cupcakes.

Warm air, fragrant with the aroma of freshly ground coffee, greeted them. The busy lunch period was over, and only a few tables were occupied.

The café, formerly a blue-plate-type diner, had been given a makeover a few years ago when the previous owner hung up his apron and sold the business to a transplanted gay couple from New York. Gone were the 1970s dark wood paneling, broken ceiling fan, tattered red leather banquettes, lace curtains, and kitschy things the owner's wife didn't want in their home. Now the space was sleek and modern with stainless steel, muted colors, and flat-screen menu displays.

They chose a table by the window; Ray liked to sit there so he could keep a watchful eye on the street, and Charlotte liked it because she sought out natural light whenever and wherever she could.

"Do you know what you're having?" Ray asked.

"Just a latte, please."

"Nothing from the bakery? Cupcake? You love cupcakes."

Charlotte shook her head. "I mustn't. The scales are telling me it's time to get back to the aquafit class."

After the server took their order and left, Ray cleared his throat.

"That Brian guy. He seemed to make you uncomfortable."

"I knew him a long time ago. We had a thing. The awful truth is that I was in love with him, and I thought he was in love with me. He was different back then and looked a whole lot better. But he dumped me, to marry Lady Deborah. I've been such an idiot for all these years."

"In what way?"

Charlotte picked at the paper napkin on the table and gave a little laugh.

"This is actually rather embarrassing. I let him mean more to me than I should have and for much longer than I should have. The funny thing is, seeing him again . . . I used to hate Lady Deborah for marrying him, but all

I can think of now is that she did me a huge favor. Taking him off me and getting lumbered with him herself."

She looked at Ray and smiled.

"It didn't surprise me in the least to hear he was having a fling with Lauren. There have been rumors about his infidelities for years. I haven't worked out yet why Lady Deborah puts up with it."

"Is it hard, having to work with him this summer?"

"I don't have to work with him for long. I have to make sure he gets his costumes sorted, but I'm delegating that to Aaron so I don't have to deal with him. And then I'll go to the dress rehearsal to see that everything works and that's about it, really."

Their conversation stopped as the server approached with their order.

"Latte for the lady, and that's for me, thanks," said Ray, with an easy smile.

"So, Ray, tell me. How's the case going?"

"You know I can't answer that." He took a sip of his Americano. "But I might just give you, well, not a warning, I'm not sure what to call it, exactly—a heads up, maybe—but you may not have Aaron as your assistant much longer. The police are building a pretty tight case against him."

*

Are they indeed, thought Charlotte as she made her way along Helm Street. She'd declined Ray's offer of a ride

back to the hotel, reminding him that she liked walking—
although she enjoyed it a lot more when Rupert was with
her—and needed the exercise. Walking past the shops
gave her a chance to see the new window displays and,
more importantly, provided a good opportunity to mull
things over. As a creative person, she often craved solitude and needed time alone with her thoughts. What
Ray had just told her about Aaron coming into focus as
a prime suspect troubled her. She walked at a brisk pace,
so deep in thought that today she barely took notice of
the shop windows. She even strode past the Uptown Silk
Shop, her favorite local fabric outlet and usually a magnet for her attention, without so much as a glance at the
elaborate display in the bowed window.

By the time she reached the driveway leading to the
hotel, vague, foggy thoughts were beginning to creep
into her mind. She walked slowly up the drive and then
quickened her step and made for the hotel's front door.
Those thoughts were evolving into a plan, but before
anything could happen, she needed to speak to Aaron.
As she entered the lobby, Aaron, who was crouching in
front of a table with his back to her, ignored the sound
of the opening door, but Harvey Jacobs looked up from
the reception desk. His face started to break into a professional greeting smile, but when he saw who it was, the
smile faded.

"Oh, Charlotte, it's just you."

"Yes, only me, I'm afraid. Sorry to disappoint you."

"No, I'm sorry. I didn't mean it like that. It's just that we're expecting a couple to check in, and I thought that you might be them." As he finished speaking, the door opened, and the three of them turned toward it. Aaron stood up and greeted the well-dressed couple that entered. They looked around with uncertainty and walked slowly across the lobby, taking in their surroundings. The woman looked up at the man, gave her head a little shake, and clutched at his arm. *There's no way I'm spending the night here*, the gesture said. Charlotte's heart sank.

They approached the desk and exchanged a few quiet words with Harvey Jacobs. Charlotte heard them say "sorry" several times, and the couple then turned around and left.

"A nice young Canadian couple," Harvey said. "Sudden change of plans and they won't be staying here after all." He shrugged. "Too bad. They were booked in for three nights."

"Well, at least they have to pay for the one night," said Aaron. "You have to cancel by three p.m. to get a refund." Harvey shuffled from one foot to the other and did not meet his nephew's reproachful gaze. Aaron groaned. "You didn't! You did, didn't you? You agreed to refund them for tonight."

"Well, I felt I had to," said Harvey. "They're just a young couple starting out, and it seemed like the right thing to do."

"We've really got to do something to turn this around, Harvey," said Charlotte, as Aaron nodded. "This lobby is your guests' first impression. It's too dark and old-fashioned. In this light, it looks just awful, and it looks even worse in full daylight. Now, I've suggested that Aaron come up with a few inexpensive ideas to lighten things up. A fresh coat of paint in a neutral color will do wonders. We've got to get the lobby sorted before the season starts, or there very well may not be a season."

"Oh, there will be," said Harvey. "There definitely will be. We've seen a big increase in the number of bookings since the, er . . ." he looked to Aaron for support.

"Since Lauren was murdered here," said Aaron with all the bluntness of youth.

"Yes, well," said Harvey. "I was looking for a gentler way to say it, but, yes, since, well, the unfortunate incident."

"Speaking of that," said Charlotte, "I've been thinking that you ought to give a little party for the theater company. The actors and stage crew."

"Oh, we don't have the money for parties," Harvey replied instantly. "They'll expect things to eat and drink, and we couldn't possibly afford that."

"Harvey, you can't afford not to do it," said Charlotte. "You must realize morale is very low just now. And after what happened, I'm sure several actors are thinking of quitting the company."

"They are?" said Aaron. "I hadn't realized—" He was interrupted by Charlotte sliding her foot across the floor and giving his foot a hard enough nudge to bring him up short. He cleared his throat. "I hadn't thought of that," said Aaron, "but yes, a reception seems like a very good idea."

"Does it?" said Harvey. "What makes you think that?"

"Well, the morale is low, you see," said Aaron, "and er . . ."

"What Aaron's trying to say," interjected Charlotte, "is that the season hasn't even started yet—we're well into rehearsals—and a cast member has been murdered. Now, she may not have been very popular, disliked even, but nevertheless, the situation is creating instability and fear amongst the company, and it would be too bad if any of the actors decided to leave now. Simon's already got to recast Lauren's roles, and if other cast members choose to leave at this late date, well . . ." She let her voice trail off as she raised her hands in a gesture of resignation and defeat.

"Yes, I see what you mean," said Harvey.

"So I suggest you view the cost of a few bottles of wine and some cheese and crackers as an investment in the goodwill from the actors that you need to make this season happen." Aaron nodded vigorously as she drove the point home. "Now then, let's set the date, and the sooner the better. We can put up notices in the backstage area."

"Well, I don't know," said Harvey. "I guess I'd have to discuss it with Nancy. See what she thinks."

"No, you don't need to talk to Nancy," said Aaron. "We'll decide the date right now, and then you tell Nancy when the party will be and she'll organize it." Charlotte gave him a quick thumbs-up.

"Er, well, I'm not sure," said Harvey. "Let me think."

"Friday evening would be good," suggested Charlotte.

"But that's tomorrow!" protested Harvey.

"Exactly," said Charlotte. "The staff needs encouragement now, not two weeks from now. Aaron will be in to see you first thing in the morning to sort things out. Let me see. He'll need a complete cast list, oh, and the backstage people, too. You know, the ones who change the sets and see to the lighting."

"When does Nancy start?" Aaron asked.

"She was supposed to start Monday. I've got lots of things lined up for her to do. She needs to get started on the filing and tidying up. But maybe she'd agree to come in tomorrow just to help out with the party."

"That would be perfect," agreed Aaron. He shot Charlotte an approval-seeking, raised eyebrow. She pinched her lips in a hint of a conspiratorial smile and gave him a quick nod.

"Well, Harvey, if Aaron's finished here for now, we've got a couple of fittings to do, so we'd best be off."

In the hallway that led to the hotel's rear entrance and backstage area, Aaron turned to her.

"What was that party idea all about?"

"I thought it might be interesting to bring everyone together so we can get a good look at them all," she said. "After all, one of them's probably our killer."

"Do you really think so?"

"I do. And here's what I think we should do—" She stopped speaking as two actors advanced toward them.

"Oh, Charlotte, there you are," one of them said. "We turned up for our fitting, but the door was locked. Did we get the time wrong?"

"No," she said. "It was us. We apologize. We were having a little chat with Aaron's uncle and were delayed." She unlocked the door to the costume department and indicated that the two should enter ahead of her and Aaron.

"I'll tell you what I've got in mind when we're finished here," she said to him.

"Before we go in, there's something I've got to tell you," Aaron said. He looked at her with earnest eyes. "Our fabric scissors. I can't find them. I think they've gone missing."

"Oh, no," said Charlotte. "They're the best pair I've ever had. Been using them for years." She made an impatient little gesture. "All those people in here after the incident . . . you don't suppose someone nicked them, do you?"

Aaron shrugged. "I don't know. Just thought I'd tell you, in case they don't turn up soon and we need to replace them."

Charlotte sighed. "Well, come on. We'd better get in there. Can't keep these two waiting any longer."

Half an hour later, their measurements taken and fittings completed, the two actors were on their way. Aaron checked his watch. "I'd better not be late. My aunt likes me on time for dinner."

"I won't keep you. But I want to give you something to think about."

"Fire away."

"You said you were afraid that your uncle might have had something to do with Lauren's murder. It can be very difficult to admit to ourselves that someone we thought we knew might be capable of something beyond what we . . . well, maybe we didn't know that person as well as we thought we did." She peered at him and he acknowledged the truth of what she was saying. "Right." She crossed her arms. "So here's what I'm thinking. If you're afraid the police are going to think your uncle was involved, then the best thing we can do is find out who did kill Lauren. If you're really sure it wasn't Harvey, that is."

She watched carefully for his reaction. His left eye twitched a little. She could hear the wheels grinding in his brain as he processed what she had just said and tried to formulate the best response. But what was the best response? The truthful one? Or, if the police were right, the one that would point suspicion away from himself?

"Me? I don't know anything about how to solve a crime. Why would I want to do that? Wouldn't it be best to just leave it up to the police? They've got DNA testing and forensics and all that stuff you see on TV."

"True. But sometimes I think they get to like the idea of one particular person as a suspect and they focus on that person, and then they get a bit selective about the evidence, so everything fits neatly together and they can get things wrapped up quickly." Aaron did not look at her, but kept his head down as he rolled up tape measures and arranged rulers in a neat row on the edge of the cutting table.

"I wouldn't know where to start," he said slowly.

"I've got a couple of ideas," Charlotte said. "I'll help you, if you like."

"What would we have to do?"

"Well, first we observe everyone very carefully at the party. See if we can pick up anything about Lauren. People tend to let their guard down at parties; they have a few glasses of wine and talk just a little more freely." Aaron nodded slowly.

"So we eavesdrop," he said.

"We do. Or rather, you do. Because you'll be the one passing round the little canapés or whatever and refilling wine glasses. And nobody ever pays any attention to the waiter."

"I will?"

"Yes, you will."

"And there's something else you need to do, and you need to do it tonight."

"What?"

"I want you to find out from your uncle who cleans that rehearsal room the detectives from the state bureau are using as their, what do you call it, something room."

"Incident room?"

"That's it."

"What do you mean 'clean'?"

"At night. After the detectives have gone home. Who cleans the room? There must be coffee cups and sandwich wrappers all over the place. Bins that need emptying, surfaces that need dusting. You know, that sort of thing."

He tilted his head.

"Sorry, you've lost me."

"If we could have a look around the room after they've gone home, we might learn something."

"Are you crazy? You want me to go in there and snoop around the police room? What if I get caught? Anyway, I doubt that there'd be anything to see. They probably use laptops that they take home with them or lock up somewhere, and there'll be a massive shredder bin. There won't be any confidential files loaded with clues just lying around waiting for us to come along, you can bet on that. They'll have all the good stuff at their headquarters in Albany or wherever."

"You're probably right, but still, ask your uncle about the cleaning arrangements. If cleaners go in, find out who and what time. We need to take a look around and see if we can find anything."

"We? Oh, jeez, I'm not sure I like the sound of that."

"Just find out from your uncle. This evening. And then call me."

Chapter 19

It was just coming up to eight o'clock when Charlotte's phone rang. She listened for a few moments, thanked the caller, and hung up. She'd had her dinner and had been comfortably stretched out on the sofa with Rupert getting ready to watch a reality cooking show. She admired the contestants' quick thinking skills. She'd be standing there poking about in the fridge trying to work out what to do with the mystery ingredient, and by the time she'd had a not-very-good idea, the allotted cooking time would be up. She set the DVR to record the show, slipped on her dark raincoat, and stepped out into the night. The air was cold and sharp but felt oddly fresh and welcome on her face. She hurried across to the hotel, unlocked the back door, and slipped inside.

"Oh, there you are. Good," she said when she saw Aaron waiting for her in the backstage area. "Where did you tell Harvey you were going?"

"I told him I'd left my laptop in your office and was going to get it, so I can't be gone too long."

"Let's go then." They hurried down the hall to the rehearsal room. Charlotte stood to one side as Aaron unlocked it, but when he went to enter, she put a hand on his arm and shook her head. "No," she said in a low voice. "You wait in the hall and keep watch. I doubt anyone will come, but just in case."

She entered the room, leaving the door open a fraction, and switched on the light. *Damn*, she thought. *I should have brought a flashlight like they do in the movies. Ray would have.* The room, reserved for table reads in the earliest stage of rehearsal, was the size of a modest boardroom, with a large oval-shaped table in the center. Chairs were grouped around it; some had been pushed in, others were pulled out and at an angle to the table as if the occupant had just got up. A couple of paper coffee cups had been left on the table, but the room wasn't nearly as messy as she'd thought it would be. As Aaron had predicted, there weren't any computers or much paper lying about.

The large whiteboard at the end of the room caught her attention. She hadn't seen it in this room before, so she assumed it belonged to the police. A white sheet that almost reached the floor had been draped over it. She lifted a corner and pulled it out and up as far as she could. A large black-and-white photo of Lauren, probably a publicity still, sat in the center of the board, with black lines drawn from her to other photos: Brian, Aaron, Harvey, and Simon. Were these men the prime suspects? Under each photo, notes had been handwritten in black marker, but she had trouble reading the words, which were somewhere between scribbled and printed. Long lines with arrows on the end connected the photos. While she was trying to work out the significance of the photos and their interconnecting lines, a tap on the door made her turn her head in that direction. Aaron hissed her name and then reached in and switched off the light. The door closed quickly and the key turned in the lock. In the windowless room, she found herself plunged into total darkness.

She reached out both hands and, touching the whiteboard in front of her, moved her hands along it until she felt the edge. Holding on to it with her right hand, she sidled around it and just managed to squeeze between it and the wall as a key turned in the lock and a second later, the overhead fluorescent lights flickered to life.

She held her breath, certain that the sound of her hammering heart would surely reveal her presence to the person who had just entered.

"It would have been safe here until morning, you know," said a male voice.

"Yeah," a woman replied. "But you know how it is. We can't live without our phones, can we?"

"Do you sleep with it?" the first voice said. The woman gave a feeble laugh, and Charlotte covered her mouth.

The only reply was the sound of chair legs being dragged along the carpet. Charlotte assumed that was the sound of the woman pulling out the chair where she'd been sitting to check it for her phone.

Charlotte pressed her back against the wall and exhaled slowly through tightly pursed lips. There is something so clandestine, so forbidden about hiding while others go about their business unaware someone is watching or listening. She found the situation distasteful. But worse, she feared what would happen if she were caught. There was nothing she could say to explain her presence in a way that would sound remotely believable. First, they'd ask what she was doing there, and second, they'd demand to know how she got into the locked room. And it wouldn't take them long to work out who had keys.

The ping of an incoming text startled her. She reached into her pocket and switched off her phone.

"Did you hear that?" the man asked. "Mmm. Hear what?" said the woman. She sounded distracted, and Charlotte thought she was probably checking messages on the phone she'd just recovered.

"That noise. I thought I heard someone's phone. It came from over here." *Oh, here we go*, Charlotte thought, as his voice came closer. She was almost prepared for discovery when the woman spoke.

"Let's go. We've wasted enough time here for one night. I'd buy you a beer on the way home, except you're driving."

Desperately wishing there was something she could hold on to, Charlotte held her breath and tried to lock her knees in place. After what seemed an eternity, she sensed him moving away.

"Ready?" the woman said, this time with more than a touch of impatience. "Let's go. I want to get home."

"Sure there's nothing else you've forgotten?" the man said. His voice sounded a little further away.

"Nope. I just wouldn't have slept very well worrying about my phone," the woman said. "I was sure I'd left it here, but all the same, I just wanted to get it. I feel better knowing I have it. You know how it is."

From the distance in their voices, Charlotte could tell they had almost reached the door.

"It'll be good when we get the one missing piece that wraps this case up for us," the man remarked. The woman did not reply. "In every case, there's always that one thing that ties it all together," he added.

"Are you talking about the weapon?" the woman asked. "We can build a stronger case against him when we have that. It's too bad the search didn't turn up anything."

The man said something Charlotte didn't catch as they closed the door and locked it behind them.

She stood frozen in place, afraid to move. As she was about to emerge from behind the white board, the sound of the key turning in the door startled her. Thinking it must be Aaron, she stepped out from her hiding place just as the door opened about six inches and a hand reached in and flicked the light switches off. Then the door closed and the key turned in the lock once again.

Her knees finally gave way and her legs dissolved as she lowered herself to the floor, resting there, legs tucked under her. There wasn't enough room for her to crawl behind the whiteboard; if they came back now, they would see her. But so be it—she couldn't stand. Her jellied knees were gone.

But the police officers didn't come back, and a few minutes later, she gathered her strength and, pushing herself up from the floor, managed to stand up. Her breathing was more normal now, the wild wringing of her heart was subsiding, and she could almost feel her adrenaline level dropping. But her mouth was so dry that her teeth felt glued to the lining of her cheek.

She reached out until she felt a chair with her right hand. She put her left hand on it and with both hands worked her way up the back of it until she reached the table. She swung her hand back and forth over the table until a soft thud told her that she'd found what she was looking for.

She could tell as she unscrewed the cap that the bottle had been opened, but she didn't care. It felt about half full, and not caring that it was lukewarm and had belonged to someone else, she gratefully drank deeply. When she'd finished, she screwed the top back on and deliberated whether to put the empty bottle back on the table or take it with her. She held on to it and then carefully, mindful that some chairs had not been tucked in, she groped her way down the table length, chair back by chair back, until she reached the end of it. With both hands stretched out in front of her like a sleepwalker, she aimed for the beckoning band of light under the door that seeped in from the hallway. A moment later, she reached the door and placed her ear against it, straining to listen. She heard nothing. She placed her hand on the doorknob and tried to turn it, although she knew perfectly well it was locked.

She leaned against the wall, trying to think, as the darkness pressed on her. *Please, Aaron*, she thought, *open the door.*

And then, as if in answer to an unspoken prayer, a key turned in the lock and Aaron's face appeared. Thrusting the empty water bottle into his hand, she shot past him and raced down the hall.

A few minutes later, she emerged from the women's washroom to find Aaron lounging against the wall, waiting for her.

"Did you lock the rehearsal room?" she asked.

He nodded. "Did you learn anything?"

"Well, maybe," she answered. "They seem to think the case hinges on finding the weapon. But tell me about when the police officers came. Where were you and what did you do?"

"I heard them coming before I saw them. They were talking, and just before they turned the corner, I warned you and locked the door. Then I just walked past them in the hall and waited in your office for them to leave. They were in there about five minutes, and when they walked by, I waited a bit longer to make sure they'd gone, and then I came back and unlocked the door for you."

"Did you hear anything interesting?" Charlotte asked.

"Not really. They were just talking about stuff."

"Stuff! What kind of stuff?"

"The woman said she hoped this case wouldn't drag on much longer. She doesn't like working late."

"Well, that's understandable. Who does? Anyway, you'd best get back upstairs. Your uncle will be wondering where you've got to. Oh, did you lock up my office?"

"Of course. There are strange people on the loose."

Charlotte laughed.

"Oh," said Aaron. "I almost forgot. You asked about how the room gets cleaned."

"The room?"

"The rehearsal room the police are using. It's cleaned during the day when police officers are there. Not like a normal office that's done at night."

"Well, that makes sense. I hope they won't miss the water bottle."

"Wasn't that yours?"

"No. I was just that parched, I took it and drank it. Someone must have left it behind."

"Eew."

"I was that desperate."

As she trudged home, Charlotte considered the photos she'd seen on the police whiteboard and tried to work out what the police thought about them.

Brian Prentice. Well, she could see a motive for him. Perhaps Lauren had threatened to tell his wife they were having an affair. But what she couldn't see was Brian actually killing her. She doubted he could have been sober enough for long enough to plan something as complicated as a murder or that he had anything like the will or determination she imagined would be required to actually carry out such a crime.

Aaron she could see, reluctantly. He hated Lauren and blamed her for bullying his cousin to death. And the police seemed very focused on the time between when Simon sent him out to get water and when he returned. So it looked as if he had opportunity and motive.

But Simon? She knew of no reason he would be on the shortlist of suspects. As far as she knew, Lauren's death was an inconvenience—now he had to find a replacement for her. A complication and distraction he didn't need just at the moment, so what possible motive could Simon have? And also, from everything she'd seen, Simon had been nothing but kind and helpful to Lauren. He'd cast her in the part and treated her well.

Harvey? Well, murder can sometimes be good for business, but not always. Ask any real estate agent trying to sell a house where someone was murdered. Generally speaking, people just don't like death all that much.

A few minutes later, she unlocked the door to her bungalow and, after enjoying the bottom-wiggling greeting from Rupert, switched on the light. Still thirsty, she pulled a pitcher of water from the fridge and poured a tall glass. As she took a long sip, her thoughts returned to the list on the police whiteboard. For the names to be there, she thought, the police must not have been able to eliminate them from their inquiry. Maybe the men on that list just hadn't been interviewed yet. Maybe they didn't have a decent alibi. She set the glass on the counter and moved into the sitting room.

One name, though, that she would have expected to see there, wasn't on the list. And that name was Lady Deborah. After all, when a man's mistress gets killed, wouldn't his wife be high on the list of suspects? There was nothing new about that particular crime, fueled by jealousy. But perhaps the police had already spoken to her and established her innocence. Or maybe they hadn't got around to her yet. Or maybe they thought an English aristocrat above a crime like murder. If so, obviously they'd never heard of Lord Lucan.

Charlotte had never met Lady Deborah; they hadn't moved in the same circles. Brian never told Charlotte where he and Lady Deborah had met, but she assumed it had been at some smart party in Belgravia or Mayfair. Some women from privileged backgrounds were attracted to the artistic, bohemian side of life—look at Princess Margaret, the Queen's sister, who had spent her twenties partying until all hours with musicians and actors and married society photographer Antony Armstrong-Jones in 1960 when she was twenty-nine.

Brian had simply told Charlotte in a halting, embarrassed way that he was finished with her and that he was going to marry Lady Deborah Roxborough. And just like that, it was over. She'd seen photographs of her replacement in British newspapers and magazines like *Country Life* and *The Lady* over the years and knew what she looked like. And more important to Charlotte, she could see how she dressed. Camel hair and Burberry coats. Launer handbags and Liberty scarves. Pearls. Understated stud earrings of precious stones. Nothing showy or vulgar: just classic good taste and superb quality that would last for years. And almost always mentioned in the articles were the Roxborough jewels—a fabulous collection that came into the family when the present Lord Roxborough's great-grandmother, Helen, an American heiress to a candy-making fortune, married the ninth earl in the 1920s. Helen was one of a cluster of rich American girls, known as "dollar princesses," who married into the British aristocracy in the early twentieth century.

At the heart of the collection was the magnificent Philadelphia suite: a diamond tiara that could also be worn as a necklace, and a pair of drop earrings. In the 1970s, the set had been modernized and the earrings broken up to form a smaller pair and a brooch. These were divided between two sisters-in-law, with Lady Deborah's mother taking the brooch.

Charlotte wondered if Lady Deborah would come to the staff party and hoped she would. It had been difficult for Charlotte to let go of Brian and move on, but now she was discovering that life takes an interesting turn when the one you thought was your enemy turns out to be your friend, even though she may not be aware of it.

And she had no doubt that Lady Deborah would be interested in meeting her, too, although she would likely feign complete disinterest. But Charlotte knew women and how curious they always are about the past loves of their husbands and boyfriends.

Charlotte checked her watch. Still early enough to ring Ray to tell him about the staff party and to invite him to come with her.

"It might be nice for you to see everybody all together in one place," she said.

"Oh, like in the old movies," he replied, "when the detective brings all the suspects together and then announces who the killer is."

She laughed. "Not quite there yet, though, are you?" No, he'd had to admit. They were not. *Good*, she thought. *Then Aaron and I still have a bit of time to see what we can find out.*

Chapter 20

"Right, then, young sir," Charlotte said to Aaron the next morning as they sat in her office. "Why don't you tell me what you were doing during that period of time at the rehearsal when Simon called a break and sent you to get him a bottle of water. How long were you gone? The rehearsal was held up while everyone waited for you to get back. He thinks you were gone longer than you should have been." Charlotte stood over Aaron, arms crossed, with a firm, clear look in her eye. He said nothing, and did not meet her gaze. "Look, Aaron, if there's something going on, and you need someone to confide in, you can tell me. In fact, if it's tied up in this Lauren business, it's probably best you do tell me. I might be able to help."

"I was smoking a joint," he said finally. "But please don't tell my uncle."

"Is that all?" Charlotte laughed lightly. "And as for your uncle, I'd be surprised if he doesn't already know that you smoke pot. But he's got more important things on his mind right now, so I doubt that he cares. And I certainly don't." A moment later, she added, "As long as you're not driving, of course."

He shook his head. "You can understand why I didn't want to tell the police that."

"Why would you have to tell the police that?"

"Because that's what I was doing when Simon sent me out to get his water. There was a lot going on, and I was feeling kind of stressed, so I thought I'd just have a couple of quick tokes." He made a little open gesture with his hand. "Just to take the edge off things. And then I still had his water to get. That's why I took a bit longer than I should have."

Charlotte mulled this over. "So that's what you were doing when Simon sent you out to get his water." She made a little jabbing motion in the air with her index finger. "That's it! That's what I heard that got me thinking. Simon sent you to get water. He sent you on that errand, so you couldn't have known he was going to call a break."

Aaron looked confused. "No, of course I didn't know. No one did. The break just sort of happened because Peter asked if he could put his script down and try out his Romeo lines off book."

"And yet," Charlotte said, "someone must have been there who took advantage of that unexpected break to kill Lauren. An opportunist, ready to strike. Or possibly, someone who had no idea he was going to kill her, saw an opportunity, and then just acted on a cruel impulse."

"Oh, is this going to be one of those cases that comes down to timing like you see on TV?" said Aaron.

"It very well might," said Charlotte. "The police are really looking at who had the opportunity. Do we know who just happened to be in the right place at the right time?"

"Not Lauren, that's for sure. Definitely the wrong place at the wrong time for her."

"It was," Charlotte agreed. "And the weapon. We have to learn more about that. What was it? Where did it come from? And where is it now? The police would like to know that, too.

"Now, about the smoking. When the police ask you where you were, why don't you just say you were outside grabbing a quick smoke? You don't have to tell them what you were smoking, do you?"

"No, I guess I don't."

"I'll tell you one thing, though. I'm kicking myself for not going to that rehearsal. Of all the ones to miss!"

"I don't think you could have done anything to prevent her death," said Aaron.

"Well, no, probably not, but I might have seen something. Nobody else seems to have done." She shook her head. "It makes you wonder how something like that could happen right in front of so many people and yet nobody notices anything."

"Maybe they did notice something," Aaron said, "but they just didn't realize that what they saw was important."

"You might be right," said Charlotte. "I wonder if there was someone there that day who didn't belong. I don't suppose you noticed any strangers when you were outside smoking, did you?"

Aaron shook his head. "No, I didn't see anybody. Well, just that lady putting her bags in her car. Brian's wife. That Lady What's-her-name. Lady Diana?"

"Lady Deborah." Charlotte didn't bother reminding him to try to get her name right.

"Yeah. Her. I wonder what she does all day. This just seems like such a weird place for someone like her. Not much for her to do."

"She goes into town most days, I think," Charlotte said. "Drives to Rhinebeck and catches the train from there. She probably does pretty much here what she'd be doing at home in London. Meeting a friend for lunch. Shopping. Only here it's Barneys instead of Harrods." She thought about that for a moment. "Although maybe at home, she'd be doing some volunteer work. Still, there's no reason why she couldn't help out here with a good cause if she felt like it." She shuffled a few papers on her desk. "Animals, probably. Women of her class almost always like animals. Horses and dogs." She glanced down at Rupert, who'd come to work with her, and was now asleep in his basket beside her desk. A small smile lit up the corners of her mouth. Then she turned her attention back to Aaron, who hovered near the door.

"What is it?"

"I'm supposed to meet with Nancy this morning about the party tonight."

"Well, you'd better get your skates on then. Nancy's not the kind of person you want to keep waiting. You're going to be very busy. Be sure to place your order with the wine shop. But I'm sure Nancy will tell you everything that needs doing. If I know her, she'll have a very long to-do list for you." Charlotte laughed as Aaron, scowling and frowning, prepared to leave. "And don't slam the door," Charlotte told him. "If you wake up Rupert, you'll have to walk him."

Aaron closed the door quietly behind him.

Chapter 21

"Oh, I'm sorry you can't make it," Charlotte said as she sipped a midafternoon cup of tea at her desk. "Yes, of course I understand, but I was looking forward to seeing you this evening." She listened for a few minutes. "Really? Well, that's interesting, because Aaron mentioned that our fabric shears have disappeared. Fairly heavy ones, with silver handles. Expensive, too, I might add." After another pause to listen, she added, "Right. Of course I will."

She ended the call and turned to Aaron, who'd returned from his meeting with Nancy in a very bad mood and was sitting beside her, peering at his phone. "That was Ray. The autopsy report on Lauren Richmond suggests the weapon wasn't a knife but a pair of scissors. I had to tell him our fabric shears are missing. He wants me to call him if ours turn up, but they could be the murder weapon. So that's not good."

Aaron's mouth dropped open as a flash of something like surprise filled his eyes. He said nothing, so Charlotte continued, "Oh, and he also said that something's come up and he can't make the party tonight, so that's one less for your guest list."

Aaron groaned. "I didn't realize how much it takes to put on a party that wasn't supposed to be very complicated." He showed her a document covered in a typed, single-spaced list. "Nancy made up the shopping list, phoned it in, and will pick up the orders this afternoon. I have to be in the lobby at four to start setting up everything."

"You got off lucky," said Charlotte. "Nancy did all the thinking for you." She lifted the tape measure from around her neck, coiled it up, and set it on her desk. "Well, I'm going to take Rupert home now and get changed. I'll see you in the lobby and give you a hand with the set up. Between the two of us, it shouldn't take long. Just make sure there's plenty of ice so we can chill the wine."

Aaron gave her a fleeting but grateful smile and tapped a reminder into his phone. Charlotte still wasn't used to that. She preferred to work from a list on paper, but in the end, what did it matter how he remembered, as long as he did and the white wine was cool?

*

With the overhead lights dimmed so the soft glow of table lamps had a faint chance of banishing the lobby's shabbiness to the corners for the evening, the room looked a bit better. Pacing nervously, Harvey waited to greet his guests. Nancy had briefed Aaron on how to serve the drinks, so he stood to one side holding a tray filled with glasses of red and white domestic wines. It was good to have an occasion to get the wine glasses out again, Nancy had said as she reminded him he would have to take them to the kitchen with plenty of time before the party started so they could be run through the dishwasher. He had added that to the endless to-do list. But somehow, he'd managed to get through everything, changed his clothes, and here he was, clean wine glasses and all.

And then, in the way of all parties, the room went from silent and almost empty to noisy and nearly full. The young cast members, chatting happily, piled in and helped themselves to glasses of wine. Sensing that his event was off to a good start, Harvey relaxed and smiled.

"The hotel is a little out of the way up here," Charlotte reminded him. "Most of them are young, and they do need excitement. There just isn't a lot for them to do. They've given up a lot to be here. Clubs, friends, family, and so on." Harvey nodded his agreement.

"Do you think I should say a few words?" he asked.

"In a few minutes. And a very few words."

"Will your police officer friend be joining us?" Harvey asked. "Ray, is it?"

Charlotte shook her head. "No. Something came up at the last minute, so he can't make it, I'm afraid."

"Probably just as well," said Harvey. "In light of what happened, his being here would probably put a damper on things. He wouldn't mean to, of course. But having a police officer here tonight while the case is still unsolved, well, it would be . . . oh, never mind." His voice trailed off as conversation stopped and all eyes turned toward the door. Brian Prentice and Lady Deborah had arrived. They paused in the doorway, cool, practiced smiles in place, just long enough to bask in their fellow guests' interest and absorb the room's goodwill and energy.

They've got so used to that kind of attention, thought Charlotte, *they consider it their due. They expect it.* Yes, Brian earned it—his theater work made him recognizable and gave people a reason to admire him—but her? Besides being born with a title, what had she ever done to deserve recognition?

The couple scanned the room until they spotted Harvey and then threaded their way through the little crowd in his direction. Charlotte straightened slightly and braced herself. Harvey reached up to straighten his tie, realized he wasn't wearing one, and shot Charlotte a panicked look.

"When they get here, you acknowledge her first," Charlotte whispered. "She's the titled one."

"Good evening, Harvey," boomed Brian. "Good little party, eh?"

Harvey nodded and turned to Lady Deborah. "Good evening Lady, er, Mrs. Prentice."

Charlotte winced. *I should have briefed poor Harvey,* she thought. Like most Americans, he was unfamiliar with the intricacies of titles within the British aristocracy and had got her name wrong. As the daughter of Lord Roxborough, she would be addressed as Lady Deborah. Charlotte gave Harvey a quick nod and sent herself a mental reminder to explain it all to him later.

"You must be Charlotte Fairfax," said Lady Deborah. "I've heard so much about you. We finally meet."

Tempted to respond, "I'm sorry . . . and you are?" Charlotte smiled and accepted Lady Deborah's proffered hand. It was limp and slightly moist. "Yes, I am," she said. "It's a pleasure to meet you after all this time, Lady Deborah."

"I'm so sorry, I've been meaning to call on you. I'm sure we'll have plenty to talk about over the next little while. I plan to be here most of the summer. You've been here quite a bit longer than that, I take it." Her eyes took in Charlotte's face, drifted down to about chest level, and then returned to meet Charlotte's steady gaze. "You'll have to tell me what there is to do around here. Besides the theater, I mean. I've had more than enough of that, and besides, it doesn't involve me. Do you not find it rather dull here?"

"I find it rather peaceful and relaxed, actually," said Charlotte in a tone a degree frostier than she intended.

"There's a small cinema—a converted church—that shows new films. Not the blockbuster kind, but the small art-house kind. Sometimes a documentary. Or quirky little British ones. There's a showing every evening at seven thirty. But once you've seen the film, that's it for a week or two."

"Oh, that's interesting," said Lady Deborah, glancing over Charlotte's shoulder. "And I suppose you get your exercise by walking everywhere."

"I have a dog, so yes, I do walk a lot. But there's also a yoga studio and a community swimming pool. A lot of fairly well-to-do retired baby boomers live in the towns around here, and they want places to exercise."

"Swimming!" said Lady Deborah. "Oh, what a lovely idea. I used to adore that. Haven't been in ages. Must get a bathing costume next week. I'm sure they'll have a pamphlet or something at the pool that'll let me know the hours."

As Aaron approached with his tray of wine glasses, Brian's eyes lit up and he raised a hand. Aaron raised the tray in his direction, but with a slight tip of her head, Charlotte indicated to him that he should serve Lady Deborah first. As Aaron held the tray out to her, Brian pulled his hand back just as Lady Deborah stretched hers out. She hesitated for a moment, her hand hovering between a glass of red and a glass of white, affording Charlotte a perfect view of the stunning ring on her right hand. It was a large blue stone, encircled with smaller clear stones held in place with silver-colored prongs. It looked identical to the ring Charlotte and Ray had discovered in Lauren's room the night she'd been taken to the hospital.

"That's a stunning ring," Charlotte heard herself saying. Lady Deborah glanced at it in that casual way women do and then manipulated her fingers slightly to reposition the heavy center stone.

"Yes, it is rather nice, isn't it? Belonged to my grandmother, and then Mummy wore it as her engagement ring. People say it reminds them of Diana's engagement ring, but of course we had ours first."

"Oh, of course," said Charlotte. "Diana's came from Garrard, if I remember correctly. Apparently a tray of rings was sent round to the palace, and she chose the sapphire."

"That sounds about right," agreed Lady Deborah. "Well, as the only two Englishwomen in this place, we must get together for a cup of tea very soon." She gave Charlotte a curt nod that signaled the conversation was over and then took her husband by the arm. "Come along now, Brian. You mustn't monopolize poor Harvey. I'm sure he has lots of other guests to see to."

"I was waiting for you to finish your conversation with Charlotte!" Brian exclaimed.

"Well, never mind that," his wife replied. "Is there anyone else we should speak to?"

"I want to speak to everybody! We haven't been here five minutes! I'm enjoying myself."

"We were never going to stay long, though, were we? We've said hello to Harvey and really that's all we need to do."

"But I want to stay and talk to the other actors," protested Brian. "They'll think me terribly rude if I leave without speaking to them."

"Oh, very well," said his wife. "But I can feel one of my headaches coming on, and I don't want to be here too long."

Harvey and Charlotte exchanged glances as Brian and his wife moved on. "If you'll excuse me, Harvey," Charlotte said, "I'd better circulate."

As she drifted away, Simon Dyer entered the room accompanied by a young woman. Catching Charlotte's eye, he raised a hand in greeting, and she made a beeline for him.

"Oh, Simon," she said. "Glad you could make it. Brian and Lady Deborah are just over there, and I'm sure they'd like to say hello to you."

He nodded vaguely. "Sure. But first I'd like you to meet Mattie Lane. Mattie's going to be joining us as our new ingenue." Charlotte gave her a welcoming smile. Mattie was petite, with long brown hair. She had a high forehead, deep-set inquisitive brown eyes, and a nose that was just a touch too long. With her hair swept up and curled, Charlotte thought she would look like a perfect

Victorian lady and would be well suited to costume dramas, whether television or theater.

"Hello, Mattie. Lovely to meet you."

"Mattie knows why she's joining the company at this late date," Simon said in a low voice. "And understandably, she's a bit reluctant to wear the costume that you had prepared for, ah, her predecessor." Mattie did not look at either of them, but kept a steady gaze on the other guests; one or two of them were watching her with equal interest. "So I wondered," Simon continued, "if you would consider making a new Juliet costume for her. Or perhaps you've got something else that might do. She just doesn't want to wear *that* costume, if you know what I mean."

"I do know what you mean. Leave it with me," said Charlotte. "I'll sort out something. Mattie doesn't have to wear *that* costume." She smiled again at the young woman. "Come and see us in the costume department on Tuesday. We'll measure you and create something for you I know you'll like."

As the two drifted away so Simon could introduce her to her new castmates, Lady Deborah let out a resigned sigh as her husband caught sight of the new arrival. He set his empty glass on Aaron's tray and helped himself to another. "That's your last one," warned Lady Deborah.

"Hello, my dear," said Brian, turning up his smile to full blast when Simon introduced him to Mattie. "It'll be a pleasure working with you, I'm sure. Well, bottoms up, Hattie!"

"It's Mattie, Brian," said Simon, before the two moved on to join the next group of actors.

His tray now filled with empty glasses, Aaron walked to the reception counter that had been set up as the bar. Charlotte caught up with him and helped him take the glasses off the tray and set them in the plastic box in which they would be transported to the kitchen for washing. Aaron picked up a bottle of red wine and a bottle of white.

"Here, give me that," said Charlotte, taking a bottle from him and wrapping a white napkin around it. "Did you overhear anything interesting whilst you were making the rounds?"

"No," said Aaron glumly. "Nothing."

"Well, let me cheer you up," said Charlotte. "Have you got anything on with Simon for Monday?"

"Not that I know of," said Aaron. "And even if I do, he's pretty flexible. What've you got in mind?"

"We're going into the city."

"We are?"

"Yes. First, we're going to Mood to look at fabric, and then we're going to the jewelry district. Or at least I am."

Aaron's eyes lit up. "Mood!"

"And I have a challenge for you. You're going to create a Juliet costume for our replacement actress."

"That's terrific, Charlotte! But we've got fabric here. Why would we go to Mood?"

"To see what's new and in case they've got something that's better, or more appropriate, than what we've got here."

"And why the jewelry district?"

"Because I think poor Lady Capulet deserves a nice new ring after all she's been through, don't you?"

Chapter 22

"Come on, Rupert. Finish your breakfast, there's a good boy, and then we're going for a lovely walk into town to see your friend Ray." Rupert gave her his best corgi grin and then returned to his bowl. Half an hour later, they were on their way.

The trees were silhouetted black against a grey sky heavy with the threat of rain, and a light mist skimmed the tops of the mountains that cradled the town. As they reached the bend in the road and crossed the bridge, Charlotte paused for a moment to look at the river, now so choked with leaves that it could barely flow. As the first drops of rain spattered down, they moved on and soon reached the Upper Crust Bakery. She left Rupert waiting under the protection of the green and white striped awning while she popped in for a pastry. Once they were on their way again, the white police station adjacent to the town hall came into view. Charlotte opened the door and Rupert bounded in, waggling his bottom in greeting to the receptionist, who waved them through.

The duty room was quiet on that Saturday morning, as Ray came out of his small office and reached out to take her coat. Charlotte set her bag down and unclipped Rupert, who sniffed his way around the office, making sure everything was just as he'd left it.

"I brought you a cherry Danish from the bakery," she said, holding out a little brown bag.

"Oh, great. I need that. Can I get you a coffee?"

"Yes, please."

"How was the get-together last night?" he asked as they walked to the coffee station. He held up a dark French Roast coffee pod, she nodded, and he slipped it into the machine. The coffee brewed and he handed her the cup before she replied.

"It was fine," she said carefully. "I finally met Lady Deborah. I'd been a little nervous about that, so it was good to get it over with, finally. She was asking how we keep fit around here. I told her about the swimming pool, and she said she might try it. Who knows? Maybe I'll see her at aquafit one of these mornings."

Ray smiled as he broke off a piece of his pastry. "It's great that you're planning to get back to the swimming."

"Ray," Charlotte began, "I've come to ask a favor of you. I'm hoping you can look after Rupert on Monday. We have to go into the city."

His eyes narrowed. "We?"

"Aaron and I. We need to look at some special fabrics. Well, I've probably got enough on hand, but Aaron's getting a little restless, and a trip into the city is just what he needs. The new actress playing Juliet doesn't want to wear the costume Lauren tried on. Actors can be very superstitious, so I've given Aaron the opportunity to design and make one for her. He's beyond keen."

At the mention of Aaron's name, Ray seemed to relax a little and agreed to look after Rupert. "He'll have to stay at home, though, and I'll look in on him at lunchtime. The Albany crew are still around, and it wouldn't look good to have him here."

"I think it would look very good to have him here, but never mind. He's happy at home."

They sipped their coffee as they chatted about ordinary, everyday things, and then Charlotte pulled a sketchbook out of her bag.

"About that ring we found in Lauren's room," she began. "Do you still have it?"

"I do. It hasn't been determined yet who owns it. We're working out the best way to ask Brian about it. That's going to need a sensitive approach, and we haven't spoken to him yet."

"I wonder, would it be all right if I made a sketch of it? I'd like to get something like it as a costume piece for Lady Capulet. Would you mind?"

She had thought all night about the ring she'd seen on Lady Deborah's finger, and although she couldn't have explained why she was reluctant to tell Ray about it, she just wasn't ready to.

He disappeared into his office and returned with the red Garrard box. She opened it, held the ring between her thumb and forefinger, and studied it. It looked exactly like the one she'd seen last night. She opened her book and began to sketch.

"Why don't you just take a few photographs?" Ray asked.

"I'm a designer, so I sketch," she replied. "Sketching makes you examine things closely in a way taking a photograph doesn't. With a sketch, I can capture the detail I want, and anyway, it's fun." The pencil made soft, whispery sounds on the paper. Her hair fell over her face as she sketched with light, swift, sure strokes.

He watched her until the phone ringing in his office summoned him. A few minutes later, he returned, and her heart pounding, but with a steady smile, she held up the box to him.

"Here you go, Ray. Thanks so much." She turned to Rupert. "Well, we'd better be off and leave Ray to it. Come on, let's be having you."

They waved good-bye, and she and Rupert walked slowly home. She couldn't believe what she'd just done—she'd actually taken the ring. She kept putting her hand in her pocket and wrapping her fingers around it, constantly reassuring herself it was still there. She'd find a safe box for it when they got home and, later, work out a plan to replace it in the Garrard box.

But what if Ray discovered it was missing between now and when she could put it back? What had she got herself into? Technically, she supposed she'd stolen it. And why? All she could think of, the only way she could justify it was that there'd been a murder, and for some reason she couldn't begin to explain, even to herself, she wanted in on it.

Chapter 23

The Trailways bus meanders through upstate New York, picking up and dropping off passengers in small towns, until it reaches Kingston. From there, after a short break, it departs for New York City.

So on a chilly Monday morning, at a few minutes before seven, Charlotte and Aaron waited at the Walkers Ridge bus stop by the village green, and as the bus barreled over the bridge, they flagged it down. They scrambled aboard into the welcome warmth and, as the only passengers, chose seats at the front across the aisle from each other.

"Now remember, Aaron, you'll have a budget of one hundred dollars and about an hour to shop," Charlotte said. Aaron laughed, his friendly, open face alight with pleasure.

"You sound just like Tim Gunn on *Project Runway*," he said.

Charlotte ignored the remark and continued. "And don't worry about pattern paper or trim. We've got plenty of that in our stock room."

We've got lots of fabric there, too, she thought, *but what the hell.* She then leaned back in her seat, closed her eyes, and let the rhythm of the bus gently rock her into a light sleep. About twenty minutes later, the bus pulled into Kingston, where they got off and changed buses. A few more passengers were on board the second bus, but Charlotte and Aaron still managed to find individual seats. As they sped along the New York State Thruway, the rural, woodsy landscape gradually gave way to an urban, built-up environment, and eventually the distinctive skyscraper skyline of Manhattan loomed into view. Passengers stirred in their seats and started gathering up their belongings, in preparation for arrival at the Port Authority Bus Terminal.

Charlotte and Aaron strolled down Eighth Avenue, past coffee shops and stores selling cheap souvenirs, luggage, and scarves. The sidewalk was crowded with determined New Yorkers bustling about their business. Although this was the heart of the fashion district, it wasn't until they turned down West Thirty-Seventh Street that the fashion became apparent. The buildings, most about five or six stories high, featured an occasional ground-floor showroom with sample goods for sale, while window displays on the second and third stories showcased wedding dresses and other formal attire. About halfway down the block, they entered an ordinary-looking building with very little signage.

"Have you been here before?" Charlotte asked.

"No," said Aaron, looking around the small space containing a few rows filled with bolts of cloth, and then in a lower tone, he added, "To be honest, I expected a bit more."

Charlotte laughed. "This is just a taste of what's to come. There's much more to it than this. This is just the home-decorating section. Interior designers come here for their fabrics. And I do, too, if I'm looking for a brocade. Heavier fabrics for upholstery and curtains come in very handy for cloaks."

They had arrived at Mood Fashion Fabrics. Swatches of fabric hung on kilt pins at the ends of the rows of bolts of cloth. The air was filled with that new-clothes smell.

"The fashion fabrics for clothing designers are upstairs," Charlotte said. "You go up on the elevator to the third floor, and you'll be amazed at what you see. Take your time. I'm going to leave you to browse whilst I run an errand. I'll be back in about an hour, and you can show me what you've chosen. But don't ask them to cut fabric until I get back—we'll make the final selection together."

She left him to make his way up to the third floor while she trotted the ten blocks north to the diamond district, where the highest concentration of jewelry retailers in the world bought and sold thousands of cut, uncut, mounted, and loose diamonds every day. She fingered the little box in her coat pocket containing the ring she and Ray had found in Lauren's room. She'd gone to a lot of trouble to borrow it from Ray, unbeknownst to him, and she had one chance to find out more about it. And then she had to work out how to return it.

She turned onto Forty-Seventh Street. "Consumer Alert. Do not buy from or sell to street solicitors," said a sign in a metal stand on the sidewalk. She stopped for a moment to admire a window display of loose diamonds on tiny blue velvet cushions. She sensed someone behind her and turned around.

"You want to buy diamonds, lady? Come with me." A young black man with gleaming teeth beamed at her in the friendliest way.

"No, sorry, not today," she replied. He moved on up the street, and she walked off in the opposite direction. Both sides of the street were lined with jewelry stores, and spoiled for choice, she eventually stopped in front of one. RJW Jewelers looked as good as any. The window display was filled with earrings, rings, and bracelets in every color and size of gemstone, with generous diamond embellishments. In large letters across the bottom of the window was written, "Engagement Rings." And the door was open.

A man who appeared to be in his early forties, wearing a black velvet yarmulke over dark, curly hair and a wrinkled black suit and white shirt but no tie, looked up from a worktable. He set down a tiny tool and stood up to greet her.

"Yes?" he said. "How may I help you?"

"I wondered if you could, well, not give me a proper evaluation, but just tell me approximately what this ring is worth," she said, holding out Lauren's ring. He took it from her and then picked up a jeweler's loupe and held it up to his eye. He then raised the ring to the loupe and studied it for a moment. He slowly lowered both hands, set the loupe on the table, and returned the ring to Charlotte.

"Madam, I'm sorry to have to tell you that the stones are not genuine. Although it's good work, this is costume jewelry. What my grandfather liked to call 'paste.'"

Charlotte nodded slowly, trying to work out the meaning of what he had just told her. If this ring was fake, did that mean Lady Deborah's was real? Possibly. Aristocrats and other wealthy people with precious jewelry often had copies made for insurance or security purposes; the originals stayed in a safe or the bank vault in their velvet bags and embossed leather boxes while the replicas went to the parties, with nobody any the wiser.

"I hope you were not given that ring under, how shall I say, false pretenses, on the understanding or assumption that the stones were genuine?"

Charlotte shook her head. "No, it's all right. But I think this ring might be a copy of another one. Would you happen to know who made this? Is there someone in the district who specializes in creating replica jewelry?"

He frowned and leaned toward her but said nothing.

"Well, thank you," said Charlotte. "I'm glad to know the truth of it, and I appreciate your time and expertise this morning."

"Not at all," he said, handing her a business card. "Perhaps you will come back and see me when you are in the market for a gemstone of quality."

"Yes, perhaps I will."

He remained standing at his workbench, his eyes following her as she left. He waited for a few moments, and then picked up his telephone.

"An English woman just came into the shop," he said. "She's got a ring. I don't know who she is or how she got it." He listened for a moment. "No, this is a different woman. In her late thirties, early forties, I would say. Nice looking. Dark hair, cut straight across the forehead and then all one length. She was wearing a blue coat." They exchanged a few more words and he shrugged, waving a hand in an expressive gesture. "We're a small community. One hears things. I thought you'd like to know. Not at all. Good-bye for now."

*

Charlotte returned to Mood to find Aaron waiting for her with several bolts of fabric ready for her approval. "I chose this pink silk for a bit of lining," he said, and then held up the end of a bolt of burgundy velvet. "This was my second choice." He set it down and then pointed to another one with a deeper, richer pile. "That's the one I really wanted, but it's more expensive. So I thought this for the overcoat and then this one"—he indicated a lightly patterned one—"for the dress. I've priced it out, and we can get it all for under one hundred dollars, but there won't be much, if anything, for a train."

Charlotte smiled at him. "Good choices. Let me see your sketch again." She peered at it and then fingered the fabric for the dress. "Yes, I think this fabric will hold up to your design. But how about this for an idea? We use the lining we've got in stock, and with the money saved, you can get the more expensive fabric that is your first choice."

Aaron shot her a grateful smile.

Charlotte nodded at the clerk, who began measuring and cutting. "Now all you have to do, Aaron, is make it work."

"The number of times I hear that every day," sighed the clerk, who folded the fabric and then placed it in a Mood bag.

Back on the street, Aaron looked around, asking, "What do you want to do next?"

"Well, it's still early, and we've come all this way, so I thought we'd treat ourselves to a bit of lunch and then we can either go to the Met and see what's new at the

Costume Institute—I know a few people there—or we can split up and you can meet up with a friend or whatever, and we can either go home together or if you want to go later, that's fine. Whatever you want."

Aaron thought for a moment. "I haven't made any plans to see anyone, so I'll just hang out with you."

"Good. We'll enjoy ourselves and then take the four o'clock bus home. I've left Rupert with Ray, so I don't want to be late back."

Chapter 24

It was dusk by the time the bus dropped them back at the village green. They stood on the sidewalk, organizing their shopping bags as the bus drove off, its red tail-lights disappearing around the curve in the road. After a short walk to the police station, Charlotte told Aaron to get along home and that she'd see him in the morning. Inside the police station, the receptionist had gone home and the little waiting area was empty. She rang the bell, and a moment later, Phil appeared.

"Oh, you're back," he said. "Come on in. He's waiting for you."

She followed Phil into the main room. He didn't look at her, but sat down at his desk and turned his attention to his computer. His behavior wasn't cold, exactly, but rather like a juror who can't look at the prisoner when the verdict is guilty. She had a sinking feeling that she knew what was coming, and when she entered Ray's office, she knew she was right. She'd been struggling to think of a way to replace the ring in the little red box without Ray knowing, and now she wouldn't have to. He'd cleared his desk in preparation for this conversation. There was nothing on it but the little red box.

He closed the door behind them and then gestured at the chair across from this desk. "We need to talk," he said.

Heart pounding, dreading what was coming, she sat.

He pulled his chair closer to the desk and slowly reached out and picked up the box. He snapped it open so she could see inside, its white satin lining slightly yellowed and the empty slot where the ring should be.

Unable to meet his eyes, she opened her handbag and removed a small blue box. She opened it, removed the ring, and returned it to its red Garrard box. The worthless stones put out a halfhearted twinkle under the overhead fluorescent lighting.

"I'm so sorry," she said softly. "I shouldn't have taken it, I know that. I don't know what came over me, and then I had no idea how I was going to get it back in the box without you knowing. It's almost a relief that you know."

"Why would you do a thing like that?" Ray demanded, and then, without waiting for an answer, he continued, "Have you any idea how much trouble you're in? If you were anybody else, I'd charge you with evidence tampering, but of course, I never would have let anybody else near it. The chain of custody has been broken, and if this ring turns out to be important to the case, it won't be admissible in court. I was supposed to hand over the box this afternoon to the state investigators, and thank God I checked it before I did. Can you imagine what it would have looked like if I'd given them this," he shook the box slightly, "that's supposedly been locked in a police safe, without the ring inside? When I saw the box was empty, I couldn't believe that you could possibly do such a thing. But I knew it had to be you."

She said nothing, and stared at her fingernails.

"Charlotte, look at me."

The tone of his voice startled her, and she raised reluctant eyes to meet his. His blue eyes glittered like cold steel. "Tell me. Why did you take it? And don't give me that crap about wanting to draw it so Lady What's-her-name could have a new ring."

"Lady Capulet," she said softly.

"So now tell me. Why did you take the ring? What did you do with it?"

"I took it to New York to get it appraised."

"You did what?! What the hell were you thinking?" He stood up and paced back and forth behind his desk, struggling to regain his composure. When he was seated again, his mouth twisted into a contortion of disgust. "And what if you'd lost it? Did you think of that?"

"I did, actually," she replied. "And I was terrified that I would. I had to keep reassuring myself that I still had it."

"But why? Tell me that. I don't understand what would have possessed you to do something like that." His tone was a little gentler, and she sensed he was starting to thaw and the worst was almost over.

"I don't know, really. I just had a feeling that the ring was somehow important and I . . . Well, I'm afraid that Aaron's going to be fitted up for Lauren's murder, and I wanted to prove somehow that he didn't do it." She sighed. "I'm so sorry. I haven't got a clue what I'm doing. I really don't know why I took the ring. I just found myself doing it. It was a really bad choice. So stupid of me."

"Well now we've finally got something we can agree on," Ray said. "You don't know what you're doing, and yes, it was an awful decision."

"What about you?" Charlotte asked. "What did you tell the detectives?"

"Nothing. I'll hand this over to them tonight. I knew it had to be with you, and since we'd be seeing each other this evening, I decided to talk to you about it in person rather than phoning you."

"So you didn't tell them the ring was missing?"

"How could I? I'd have looked like a total idiot for losing something that was supposed to be in a police safe. How could I tell them that I let my girlfriend look at the ring and while my back was turned, she stole it?" His voice was slightly raised, and Charlotte cringed at the harshness of the words. Seen in that light, maybe the worst wasn't over, after all. She tried to steer the topic onto more solid ground.

"And Rupert? How was he?"

"I took him for a walk about one," Ray said abruptly. "He was fine."

"Well, thank you for seeing to him." They lapsed into a pained silence filled with mistrust on one side and regret on the other, which Charlotte broke a few moments later. "Well, I guess if that's everything, I'd better get home to him. It's been a long day, and I'm tired."

Ray nodded and stood up. He checked one last time to make sure the ring was in its box, and then placed it in the safe. "I'll drive you," he said.

They said good-night to Phil as they passed his desk, and Ray held the door for her as they left the station and made for the marked police car parked out front. As they drove toward the hotel, Ray broke the silence.

"What about the ring? After all the trouble you went to, did you get it evaluated?"

"It's fake." Her voice sounded small in the darkness. "If Brian gave it to her, knowingly or not, he gave her a worthless piece of costume jewelry. What the jeweler said his grandfather would have called 'paste.'" She stole a glance at Ray's profile in the soft shadows of the car's interior lighting.

"But here's something interesting that I should have told you," she went on. "That ring is a copy of one that

Lady Deborah wore at the staff party on Friday night. You know, the party you were too busy to attend."

"Don't be like that. It doesn't become you. I'd have gone if I could, but something came up."

"Sorry."

"As a matter of fact, I was really looking forward to seeing you. I haven't seen enough of you lately and I've missed you. It's been all business. Murder inquiries do tend to take precedence over everything else. The good news for you at the hotel, though, is that the Albany boys are winding down that part of the investigation and they'll be out of there soon."

"That doesn't matter to me. What matters is us. Do you think you can forgive me?"

He reached over and touched her hand. "I already have. But it does make me wonder if I can trust you, so we're going to have to work on rebuilding that. I thought I knew you and then this. It seems so unlike you." He slowed down for the turn into the Jacobs Grand Hotel driveway. "And you have to promise me you'll never do anything like that again."

"No, I won't. Of course, I won't. But here's something else. I think the jeweler I spoke to knows something about the ring. He seemed a bit shifty."

She sighed and settled back into her seat, and a few moments later, Ray pulled up beside her bungalow.

She leaned toward him. "Call me when you can. Again, I'm so sorry."

"I know." He leaned over to kiss her, and she wrapped her arms around his neck and clung to him. "I'm on shift until eleven," he said. "I could come over when I finish work, but don't wait up for me. If I get called out, it could be late." She nodded and then reluctantly let him go. Ray waited until she was safely inside her bungalow and then put the car in reverse and drove away.

Rupert was curled up on the sofa, waiting for her return. He stood up, waggled his bottom in greeting, and accepted her pats. She was glad for the opportunity to take him outside for his evening walk. As they strolled past the bungalow where Lady Deborah and Brian Prentice were staying, a light went off in the living room, and a moment later, Brian charged out of the house.

"You stupid, bloody fool!" came a shrill shout in a refined English accent. "You've only gone and ruined everything!" This was punctuated by the melodramatic sound of a slamming door.

Ruined what, I wonder, thought Charlotte.

Brian said something in the direction of the slammed door that Charlotte didn't quite catch, and a moment later, he was on the path in front of her. As he took a step or two closer, she caught the sour smell of alcohol that was his breath. *God, he's been drinking for hours*, she thought.

"Everything all right, Brian?" asked Charlotte, mentally kicking herself for saying such a daft thing. *Why do we English always ask if everything's all right when it's obvious everything is bloody well not all right?*

"Oh, I didn't see you there. Yeah, everything's fine, thanks," Brian replied, and then he let out a barking cough that shook his shoulders. *Of course it is,* thought Charlotte. He lit a cigarette and fell into step with her. *I wish he wouldn't smoke,* she thought.

"I hear the state police are winding down their investigation here at the hotel," Charlotte said. "Have the police talked to you yet?"

"Yeah, they asked me all the usual questions." He took a deep drag on his cigarette and blew smoke into the trees above their heads. "At least, I guess they're the usual questions; I've never known anyone murdered before. 'Where were you? What was your relationship with the deceased?' That sort of thing." He pulled an old-fashioned hip flask from his coat pocket, the kind that sporting gents used to take to the races, and tipped it in her direction. She shook her head, and he took a long, hard sip ending with a satisfied "Aah." *I'll bet that flask's got a lot of mileage on it,* she thought.

"And where did you tell them you were?" she asked.

"I told them where I was. I was at home all morning, learning lines. It takes me a lot longer to learn them now than it used to, let me tell you. Deborah was there. She can vouch for me."

The thin trickle of conversation ran out, and they trudged on for a few more steps in strained, uncomfortable silence until Charlotte said, "Right, well, this is where Rupert and I leave you. We'll be heading back now. Come on, Rupe, this way."

Brian stubbed out his cigarette in the damp earth of the path.

"Right, then. See you tomorrow," came the alcohol-soaked voice out of the darkness behind her.

As she and Rupert settled in for the night, she pulled the bedclothes over her shoulder, turned on her side, and switched off the light. She lay in the dark, eyes closed, listening to the quiet night sounds outside her window, as her thoughts drifted over the moment in time that had been today. What was the significance of the two rings? And what had Brian ruined? *Probably everything he touched*, she thought, *if past experience is anything to go by*. Rupert made little snuffling noises as he drifted off to sleep. She put her arm around Rupert and thought about Ray, who she hoped would arrive soon.

Chapter 25

"Morning, Aaron. Nice to see you in here so bright and early."

He looked up as Charlotte entered, smiled, and then returned to his task. A long piece of brown pattern paper covered the worktable. He referred to a list of measurements and, using a hip ruler, tape measure, and T-square, marked off straight and curved lines with a thick pencil. Swatches of fabric were pinned to a nearby dress form.

"Oh, I've been hard at work for over an hour. Mattie's already been in, and I've taken her measurements. She wanted to get that done before morning rehearsal began."

"Oh, right." Charlotte approached the worktable. "So, tell me what you've got going on here," she said.

Aaron pointed to the paper. "I'm working on the pattern for the underdress. I thought I'd put in a high waist to make it more flowy and to give it some movement when she walks."

"Let's revisit your sketch," said Charlotte. When he handed it over, she pointed at it. "There's no high waist here. You've drawn it slightly fitted, and this will be much more flattering and period appropriate than what you seem to have in mind. And while flow and movement when she walks are good, a high waistline in this case is not." She pointed at his pattern pieces. "That's practically a Regency silhouette you've got there, and you're not making a dress for Elizabeth Bennet."

"Who?"

Charlotte laughed. "Oh, dear me. It's not your fault, Aaron, but everyone really needs to know a bit of history and literature to get on in this profession. Did they not offer a course in the history of fashion at this school of yours?"

"Next semester, I think."

"Oh, I do hope so. In the meantime, how are you coming along with that copy of *Romeo and Juliet* I asked you to read?"

Before he could answer, Simon Dyer appeared in the doorway, and Aaron shot him a grateful look for coming to his rescue.

"Oh, hello, Simon," said Charlotte. "We're just going over the details of the new costume Aaron's making for Mattie. The new girl playing Juliet."

"Yes, I know who Mattie Lane is," said Simon gently. "Listen. I need your help. We're about to start morning rehearsal, and I was supposed to meet with Brian Prentice, but he hasn't turned up. Have either of you seen him? I tried ringing his phone, but there's no answer."

"Not me," said Aaron, pulling a pencil from behind his ear and returning to his pattern.

"No, I haven't seen him this morning, but I did see him last night," said Charlotte. "He was out walking and he'd had a few." She looked from Simon to Aaron and back again. "He may be in trouble. I'll get my coat. Aaron, you come with me. Simon, you'd better give us his phone number, just in case, and we'll let you know as soon as we find out anything." She handed Simon a square of her scrap paper, and after scrolling through the numbers on his phone, he scribbled down a number and gave it to her.

Aaron and Charlotte walked down the hallway at a normal speed. When they reached the back door, Charlotte pushed down on the bar that opened it, and they crossed the parking lot and reached the walkway that led to the bungalows.

Aaron waited outside Charlotte's bungalow while she ducked in and emerged a moment later with Rupert on his leash.

"If we're going for a walk, he might as well come, too," she said as they set off. The car was not parked in its usual spot outside Brian and Deborah's bungalow.

"Here, hold Rupert and wait here while I check out the place," said Charlotte. "Maybe he's just slept in."

She ascended the three wooden steps, and after a quick backward glance over her shoulder in Aaron's direction, she opened the screen door and knocked on the dark green wooden door. She waited a moment, and when there was no sound from inside, she tried the handle. It was locked. She knocked again and placed her ear close to the door, listening for the slightest sound from within. Nothing.

She returned to Aaron and said, "I think the house is empty, but let's go round and look in the windows. The car's gone, so presumably his wife's out. For all we know, he might have fallen after she left, so let's look in the windows and see if we can spot anything."

The windows were low to the ground, and Charlotte thought, as she had many times before, how easy it would be for someone to break into one of the bungalows. The area was secluded, and the grounds had no motion-sensor lights or closed-circuit television cameras. The curtains in the living room were drawn, so they checked the bedrooms in the back. The curtains there were drawn, too.

"I expect Harvey has a set of keys to all the bungalows if we need to get in," Aaron said.

"Probably. But there's somewhere else we should look first. If he's not in the bungalow, he could still be outside, but I hope not."

"Outside?"

"Yes, I met him out here last night when I was walking Rupert. He'd had a row with Deborah, and he stormed out of the bungalow just as Rupe and I were going past. He'd been drinking. Heavily, by the looks of it. The three of us walked along the path, this way." She pointed toward a slightly more wooded area, and they set off in that direction. When they had gone a few hundred feet, Charlotte paused. "Everything looks different at night, but it was about here, I think, that we stopped, and Rupert and I turned around and went home."

She didn't say to Aaron that she hadn't been able to stand being around Brian any longer, with the awful smell of cigarette smoke that clung to him and the alcohol on his breath that was just as bad.

They looked around but saw only bare trees. The damp ground was littered with dead leaves. "Ring him," Charlotte said suddenly, handing Aaron the piece of paper with Brian's phone number on it.

"What?"

"Your phone. Call him." Aaron keyed in the number, and a moment later, they heard the tinny sound of a cell phone ringing, *Brrring-brrring*, followed by a brief pause, and then another *Brrring-brrring*. They listened intently, turning their heads in the direction they thought the sound was coming from. And then the sound stopped.

"Gone to voice mail now," said Aaron. "I think it's coming from over there, but I can't be sure. It's hard to tell." Aaron and Charlotte looked at each other, and then she unclipped Rupert from his lead.

"Okay," she said to Aaron, "try it again."

Brrring-brrring. Brrring-brrring.

"Show me!" she said to Rupert. "Where is it? Let's go! Show me where it's coming from." Rupert took off in the direction Aaron had indicated he thought the noise was coming from, and the pair hurried after him. A few yards farther on, Rupert stopped and began scratching in a pile of brown, brittle leaves with his front paws.

"What is it?" Charlotte said when they reached him. She bent over to see what Rupert was pawing at, and then picked something up in her gloved hand. She held it up to Aaron. "It's his flask. He was drinking out of this last night, so he must be nearby. Ring the phone again." They heard the ringing again, louder this time and in a better defined direction.

"You know, it might be a good idea to put Rupert on his leash now," Aaron suggested. "Just in case. We don't know what we're going to find, do we?"

"Right," said Charlotte, holding up a hand to indicate there was no need for him to say anything more. She clipped Rupert on his leash as Aaron set off, calling Brian's name. About a hundred feet away, at the bottom of a small embankment, he stopped, crouched down, and then stood up, took off his coat, and laid it on the ground. With a racing heartbeat and a hard knot in her stomach, Charlotte tied Rupert loosely to a nearby sapling and then rushed to Aaron on trembling legs.

"What is it? Have you found him?"

She, too, crouched down and clutched Aaron's arm. Brian was sprawled on his back, his head turned slightly away from them. His mouth was open slightly, his eyes half-closed.

"Is he alive?" Charlotte asked.

"I'm not sure," said Aaron.

"Give me your phone," Charlotte demanded.

"Oh, Ray, thank God you're there," she said when he answered. "We need help. Yes. Right away. I'm with Aaron in the woods beside the hotel. Brian didn't show up for rehearsal this morning, he wasn't in the bungalow, so we went looking for him. He's—"

"He's breathing!" Aaron cried. "But just barely. He's shivering a little, too."

"Yes," Charlotte said into the phone. "He's breathing, but only just. I don't think he's conscious. Yes, we need an ambulance. We need everybody." She listened for a moment. "Yes, I'll do that. Okay."

She took off her jacket and placed it over Brian.

"Ray says you're to stay here with Brian and I'm to return to the hotel driveway so I can show them the way. They don't want to waste time trying to find us."

"That makes sense," said Aaron. "I wish we had blankets for him. He's very cold, after being out here all night."

"I wonder if I've got time to fetch some blankets, then get back in time to meet the police," she said.

The distant rise and fall of sirens answered the question. "No," they both said at the same time.

"You'd better go!" said Aaron. She sprinted off but paused to look back when she reached the top of the small incline. Aaron had lain down beside Brian, holding him close, trying to warm him with his own body heat.

Legs pumping and heart pounding, Charlotte ran toward the road.

*

"He's critical, and the docs can't say at this point what his chances are," Ray said over the phone an hour later. Charlotte and Aaron had returned to the costume department after the ambulance had arrived, and they'd been keeping busy while they waited for news. "It's minute by minute. But they did say it was lucky you two found him when you did, and he's also lucky that the temperature didn't drop below freezing last night. He's got a fierce bump on his head, too."

"Oh?"

"Yes, he could have hit his head on something when he fell down that incline. There'll be lots of rocks under all the dead leaves."

Fell? Charlotte wondered. *Or was he pushed?*

"The thing is," Ray continued, "we haven't been able to contact his wife. We've been calling the number on Brian's phone. Do you have any idea where she might be?"

"Well," said Charlotte, "I know she goes into the city several times a week, so that's where she might be today. There's nothing much for her to do around here, so she escapes. But where exactly she goes, or what she does there, I don't know. Sorry. Wish I could help. If I think of anything, I'll let you know."

She ended the call and returned to Aaron's worktable, where he was drawing pattern lines on the brown pattern paper, looking very pleased with himself. He stepped back from it when she approached. "Well, what do you think?" Charlotte adjusted her glasses and peered at his work.

"Looks fine. I'm glad you're spending so much time in the preparation before cutting your fabric. 'Measure twice and cut once' works for us, too."

Aaron put his pencil behind his ear and removed a few pins from the pincushion shaped like a red tomato he wore on his wrist. Charlotte had just about managed not to laugh the first time she saw him wearing it.

Charlotte went back to her desk. A few minutes later, at the sound of a car coming up the drive, she stood up and looked out the window. It was Lady Deborah's car.

She phoned Ray, got her instructions, and put on her coat.

The day had warmed up considerably, and under ordinary circumstances, the bright sunshine would have lifted her spirits. But she wasn't really looking forward to the conversation she was about to have.

She waited while Lady Deborah got out of the car, placing her feet carefully to avoid stepping in mud.

"Hello," said Charlotte. "We've been trying to reach you."

"Oh, yes? I had my phone switched off. I was having lunch with a friend, and a ringing phone is just so rude, don't you think?"

"Probably. Except of course, in an emergency."

"And is there an emergency?" she asked, opening the back door and reaching in to pick up two colorful shopping bags.

"I'm sorry, but yes, there is." Charlotte tried to remember word for word what Ray had told her to say. "It's about Brian. He's been injured and is in hospital. The police wish to speak to you." Lady Deborah straightened up slowly, a bag in each hand.

"Oh, God. Now what's the old fool gone and done? Fallen down drunk and hurt himself, I expect."

Charlotte held out her hands for the bags. "Why don't you leave those with me, get back in your car, and drive to the police station in town. They're waiting for you, and they can answer all your questions. Or if you'd like, I can drive you."

"Is he alive?"

"Yes."

"Is he in hospital?"

"Yes. Kingston."

"Well, then I don't have any questions. And since you seem to know so much about it, why don't you just tell me what's happened, and save me the trip into town? Or if the police really want to speak to me, tell them they can come here and talk to me. People like us don't want to make a fuss."

Stunned by the dispassionate coldness of her response, Charlotte followed her to the door of her bungalow. Lady Deborah gave her an imperious look, shrugged slightly, and said, "Well, you'd better come in then."

"Good," said Charlotte. "I'd like to use your phone, if I may. I left mine in the office."

As Lady Deborah hung up her coat and then disappeared, Charlotte picked up the phone and dialed. While she waited for Ray to answer, the sound of running water came from the kitchen. *That'll be her putting the kettle on*, thought Charlotte. *There's nothing a nice cup of tea can't fix.* She turned her back to the kitchen doorway, and when Ray answered, she urged him to get there as soon as he could. He asked her to stay with Lady Deborah until he arrived.

"I'm just going to change out of these city clothes," Lady Deborah called from the kitchen. "The kettle's about to boil, and I've laid out the tea things, if you wouldn't mind wetting it."

Charlotte made the tea, slid a few digestive biscuits onto a small plate, put the whole business on a tray, and carried it through to the sitting room. She pulled open the curtains to let in some light, and then she sank into the tired brown corduroy sofa and examined her surroundings. Other than a few books stacked on a chair, a folded newspaper on a side table, and a laptop computer on the table, there were few personal possessions and no personal touches. When it was time to go, they would pick up their belongings and walk out, leaving the place exactly as it had looked on the day they walked into it, all without any of that fuss people like Lady Deborah so deplored.

Lady Deborah entered the room from the bedroom end, and perched gracefully on the edge of the chair that matched the sofa. She was wearing a soft beige cashmere sweater accentuated by pearls, a pair of dark brown trousers in a small, tasteful check, and a pair of brown loafers with the Gucci horsebit. Charlotte had to hand it her; she looked the part. If she were designing a costume for an aristocratic woman of Deborah's age, she'd dress her just like that. The effect was perfect.

"Why don't you pour?" suggested Lady Deborah. Charlotte reached for the teapot and filled two cups. "I take mine clear," said Lady Deborah. Charlotte handed her the cup and gestured at the biscuits. Lady Deborah shook her head and took a sip of tea.

"That's better," she said, with a watery smile. "Now why don't we start again, and you tell me what all this is about."

"We found Brian this morning in the grounds. He appeared to have fallen and hurt his head. He'd been out there most of the night and has been taken to hospital. I can't tell you his condition, because I don't know. The police will take you to see him, and then they will want to ask you a few questions."

"They'll probably want to know why I didn't realize he was out there," she said. "Well, that's simple. We don't sleep together and haven't for some time. Brian usually passes out on the sofa. Or the floor. Sometimes he gets himself up and sometimes he doesn't. So I didn't think anything of it when he didn't come to bed last night, because he never does. And when I didn't see him this morning, I reckoned he'd managed to get himself over to the theater for an early rehearsal." She took another sip of tea. "Theater people keep irregular hours, as you well know. Evening performance followed by hours in the bar, sleep late, get up midafternoon, do it all again." She sighed. "You wouldn't believe the trouble Brian's got into over the years because of the drinking. Countless times I thanked God the police didn't charge him, or

I don't know where we'd be. But sometimes I think it would have been better for him if they had charged him."

"Do you like it here?" Charlotte asked.

"Here? Of course not," said Lady Deborah, who seemed a little taken aback by the sudden change in topic. "It's in the middle of nowhere! The only good thing about it is the access to the city, but I'd much prefer to be in the city itself. I never did like the country, although of course, I grew up there."

Of course you did, thought Charlotte. *In a beautiful, stately home filled with priceless treasures and objets d'art that your younger brother and his wife will one day inherit.*

"I've been wondering," said Charlotte, "what you would like me to call you. Lady Deborah seems a bit formal, given the circumstances."

"Yes, these days it is," Lady Deborah agreed. "Call me Deborah, if you like, but not Deb or Debbo or any of those awful nicknames. And only you. I expect everyone else to call me Lady Deborah. Besides," she stifled a yawn, "the Americans seem to like it, although they can be overly familiar at times. They have no idea about British titles and seem to think I'm royalty! Practically the Queen, someone said! But as old-fashioned as a title might seem, it still helps if one wants to get a good table in a decent restaurant." She pronounced the word *restron*, like an odd English-French hybrid. It had been some time since Charlotte had heard that. *You're very close to overplaying the Brit abroad, Deborah,* she thought.

"Do you have lunch often in New York?" Charlotte asked, wondering if she should refer to it as *luncheon*.

"Two or three times a week, at least. I like to meet up with wives from the consulate. Apparently they're planning to hold a little reception for Brian and me to introduce us to New York society. He'd like that."

Charlotte smiled and nodded. *He'd like that? Really?* "Oh, very nice."

At the sound of an approaching vehicle, Lady Deborah stood and peered out the window. "Oh, aren't we lucky? It's that nice policeman I've seen you talking to." She reached for her handbag and pulled out a Chanel lipstick. "Let him in, if you wouldn't mind?"

Charlotte opened the door and stood aside as Ray entered. He stood in the center of the room, looking from one woman to the other. "Let's all sit down for a moment," he said. "Has Charlotte filled you in?"

"Yes, she has," said Lady Deborah. "Brian was wandering around in the woods, drunk, and got himself into trouble."

"He's severely dehydrated and hypothermic," said Ray. "They're still working on him and doing their best. He's in the hospital in Kingston, and I'd be glad to drive you there, if you wish. Afterward, I'd like to ask you a few questions."

Deborah made an exasperated little lip-smacking sound. "Oh, very well. Leave it to Brian to put everyone to all this trouble. It's all just too upsetting," she muttered. "I can feel one of my headaches coming on."

She opened her handbag and began scrabbling around in it. "Charlotte, fetch me a glass of water whilst I get ready to leave, would you?"

Charlotte returned from the kitchen with a glass of tap water just in time to catch the tail end of what Lady Deborah was saying, "—seat 'em all."

She raised an amused eyebrow in Ray's direction and sent a silent message. *Did I hear that right? Does she really think Brian's such a draw that the theater's going to sell out?*

Ray opened the door and stood to one side as the women left and then closed it behind him. As Lady Deborah started toward the car, he called her back.

"Have you got your key? I'd like to see this door locked."

"There's nothing of much value in there, but fine, if it makes you happy," she replied, pulling a key on a Statue of Liberty keychain out of her handbag and doing as he asked.

"Well, Charlotte," she said as she scanned the mountains, and then turned back to the car, "let's get together soon and go for a swim. I'm still intending to pick up a bathing costume."

Charlotte stood in the road, watching them drive off, and then, her mind working overtime, walked slowly back to her workroom, where Simon and Aaron were waiting for the latest news. Simon, worried about having to recast another actor, desperately hoped Brian would recover quickly, while Aaron went quietly back to his dress form, muttering to himself as he pinned pieces of paper on it. Finally satisfied, he stood back, folded his arms, and smiled.

Chapter 26

"Well, that is good news," said Charlotte into her telephone the next morning. "Yes, I'll let everyone know." Aaron glanced up from the sewing machine and then returned his attention to the pink fabric he was feeding with both hands through the machine.

"That was Ray," Charlotte said, raising her voice slightly to be heard above the steady stitching sound. "It looks as if Brian's turned a corner and he's going to be okay." Aaron stopped the machine.

"Well, that's good news for Simon," said Aaron, leaning forward slightly to check his work. He picked up the scissors that were meant to be used for cutting paper, gave them a skeptical look, and snipped a piece of thread. "He said the plays are coming together nicely and he dreaded having to find another old British guy to take over, because we're opening in a couple of weeks."

"I doubt those were his exact words," laughed Charlotte.

But the rapid whirring sound of the sewing machine as the needle clicked up and down drowned out her voice.

She watched for a few more minutes as Aaron finished a seam and got up to press it. She'd showed him how to do it the old-fashioned way, with a damp cloth that gave up a fragrant cloud of warm steam when the dry iron touched it. She'd explained that this method was much kinder to the fabric than placing a steam iron directly on it and provided better protection against burning the garment. He'd studied the result for a moment and decided it also gave a sharper, cleaner look. It worked especially well on a hemline, she'd told him, if you were looking for a crisp, defined look.

"Do you know who taught me that?" she'd asked.

He had grinned and replied, "No, who?"

"My grandmother. That's the way women of her generation did it."

After giving it some thought, Aaron had decided to tell Ray what he'd really been doing during the time when Lauren had been stabbed. Ray had just smiled when a nervous Aaron told him he'd been afraid to be honest about what he'd been up to because he'd been smoking a joint.

"Son, we've got a rock star drummer lives down the road, and he and his friends have been smoking Hawaiian Gold up here since the 1960s. If we won't touch him, we won't touch you. I'll tell the state police investigators what you just told me, and they may want to speak to you again at some point. We don't care that you were smoking, but the fact that you were out there does interest us. Did you see anything? Anyone who shouldn't have been there?"

Aaron had shaken his head. "No," had been all he said.

"Sure?" Ray had asked. "You just keep thinking about that. Try a little harder, and maybe you'll come up with something."

*

Charlotte smiled at the young woman behind the counter of the community swimming pool, set down two dollars to cover the cost of her swim, and moved into the women's changing room, to be greeted by the smell of chlorine and warm, humid air. She ducked into a cubicle, slid the lock closed, and started peeling off her outer clothes. The lane swim had started about ten minutes ago, and except for the cubicle beside hers, whose door was also locked, the changing room was empty. As she sat on the bench and bent over to take off her boots, a familiar voice coming from the next cubicle made her stop what she was doing and hold her breath.

"Harriette, hello, darling, it's me." Lady Deborah paused and then spoke. "No, dear, I'm not coming into town today. Well, here's the thing. I've been asked to go in and have a little chat with the police about that dreadful girl's murder and it's all just too tiresome. They'll want to know where I was a couple of weeks or so ago—as if I can remember—but it's a Wednesday they're interested in, so I must have been having lunch with you. That's what's in my diary, anyway, so that's what I'll tell them. Just telling you this in case they call you." Something about her tone puzzled Charlotte. The usual imperiousness was missing, and although the words were spoken with a certain breeziness, there was an underlying hint of . . . what? Coaxing? *No*, thought Charlotte, *close but not coaxing. More like coaching.*

"No, I can't remember the exact date, but it'll have been one of the days we were shopping at Barneys and had lunch." During the next pause, someone turned on the shower.

"No, Harriette, I don't think you were at the hairdresser that day. Look, just to keep things simple, no matter what day it was, if anyone asks, we had lunch. That's all you have to say. All right? Speak to you soon." The conversation ended, and a moment later, the lock on the cubicle door slid back. The door banged softly, and then there was silence.

Charlotte realized she was now trapped in the cubicle. She couldn't risk coming out until she was sure that Lady Deborah had left the changing room. If she did, Lady Deborah would know she'd overheard the conversation. She finished removing her street clothes, and when she was ready for the pool, she sat on the little bench in her bathing suit and flip-flops as five endless minutes ticked by.

Finally, she cautiously slid back the lock on her cubicle door. The changing room was empty. She deposited her bag of clothes in a locker, shut the door, and headed to the pool.

She slipped into the warm water, reveling in that first moment of buoyancy, and struck off with a vigorous crawl stroke down the length of the pool. She passed Lady Deborah in the slow lane, her blonde hair piled on top of her head, bobbing along in a sedate breaststroke, but ignored her and plowed on.

Charlotte loved the swimming sessions and wondered why she hadn't been in such a long time. As her arms and legs moved effortlessly through the calming water, she often used the time in the pool to think about work problems, what she would have for dinner, what she would say to her mother the next time they spoke, or what film was coming to the local cinema that she and Ray might see on a Saturday night. Today, though, her mind was filled with thoughts of Lady Deborah, who had obviously been firming up her alibi.

But why? On her little day trips into New York City, was she heading for the cheating side of town? Is that why she was asking her friend to cover for her? Because she was seeing another man? Was that what she didn't want the police to know?

Charlotte kicked off against the side of the deep end of the pool and headed back toward the shallow end, enjoying the pace she'd set for herself. She'd do a couple more lengths at this speed and then take it a little slower.

Her thoughts returned to the Lady Deborah problem. No, another man wouldn't be an issue. The Prentice marriage seemed well over; they just hadn't given it a decent burial. So if she was seeing someone in New York City, why not just tell the police, if they asked, where she was? Why bring her friend—what was her name— Harriette into it?

And the rings. What was the significance of them? And that jeweler. Did he know something? What did he know?

The ring. Something about the ring was starting to bother her. It was something someone had said. Ray? Well, he'd said lots that had bothered her, but then she'd asked for every bit of what she'd gotten. She still didn't understand how or why she'd taken the ring.

She reached the shallow end where Lady Deborah was waiting for her. Charlotte didn't want to stop her workout to talk to her, but to simply turn around and swim off would seem very rude. So she stood up in the waist-high water.

"Hello, Charlotte! I didn't wait for you to contact me, but found out the swim times for myself, and here I am. What fun!"

"Hi, Deborah."

"Are we going for a coffee?"

"I've only done two lengths, so it's too soon for me to leave. I haven't been here in ages and really want to get in a good swim."

"Oh. That's too bad."

"Sorry. Another time perhaps."

Lady Deborah, perhaps not used to being turned down, pursed her lips in a little moue of disappointment. Charlotte turned and launched herself once again into the pool and, with a nice strong kick that she hoped hadn't splashed Lady Deborah too much, disappeared toward the other end of the pool. When she returned at the end of the next lap, Lady Deborah was gone.

I guess the swimming wasn't for her, Charlotte thought. *And after all the trouble she must have taken to find a nice bathing costume.* She kicked off, headed back down the pool, and swam until she was pleasantly exhausted.

Chapter 27

The sugar maple trees on the grounds of Jacobs Grand Hotel, warmed by an increasingly bright sun and nourished by recent rains, had unfurled their brilliant green leaves of another year. The ground was firmer; gone was the boggy springiness of late winter. The lovely carpet of purple crocuses and white snowdrops had bloomed and faded, and now, as the last week of April approached, spring, with its joyful sense of wondrous renewal, was well established.

And as the days grew longer, so did Charlotte and Rupert's walks. Another of the great benefits of living with a dog, Charlotte often thought, was that if you live in the right place, the daily walks keep you in touch with nature. You get to know your area and see the changes that may not be noticeable from one day to the next but do become noticeable week by week, month by month, and year by year.

Charlotte thought again, as she did at this time every year, how much more welcome the return of spring was because of winter. Without the dreary, cold, short days that preceded them, the longer, warmer days of spring would have no special meaning. And just as spring marked the beginning of a new season for nature, it also meant the beginning of a new season for the members of the Catskills Shakespeare Theater Company. And the prelude to that was dress-rehearsal week.

"Oh, Aaron, what a lovely job you did on the Juliet costume!" The finished garment was artfully displayed on a mannequin when Charlotte entered the workroom that morning. "And with dress rehearsals coming up, we'll be able to see it in action, as it were." She rubbed her hands together. "You'll find the dress will really come to life when you see it on Mattie. Has she seen it yet? Has she been in for her final fitting?"

Grinning widely, Aaron ran a hand down the front of the undershift as if to smooth a nonexistent wrinkle and then tugged at the sleeve to straighten it.

"She hasn't been in for the final fitting, and she hasn't seen it. I hope she likes it."

"Oh, I'm sure she will." Charlotte walked around it, taking in the pale pink undershift and the softly draped sleeveless outercoat, gathered gently at the waist. "The gold braid on the bodice is a nice touch," she said, noting that it had been hand stitched without so much as one pucker, "and so is the tiny train. Just enough." She sent an approving smile in Aaron's direction. "And is there a headpiece to go with this?"

"I'm still thinking about that," he said. "It needs something to finish it off. Not sure yet what kind of hat. I thought maybe a little pillbox out of the brocade. Oh, and by the way, when is the dress rehearsal?"

"The run-through for the cast is Thursday morning, and we'll do last-minute adjustments throughout the day. Final dress rehearsal is Friday evening, and we'll both go. I'll have a word with Simon so you can see the play from front of house. You really must see the costumes on the actors, under the lights, to get a sense of whether they work. You can also tell if the costumes are right by how comfortable and confident the actor seems in them. The actor can't be fussing or worrying about his clothes. They have to support him and stay out of his way."

"That's a good way to describe what a director needs to do, too," said Simon, who had entered just in time to hear Charlotte's last remark.

"Oh, hello!" said Charlotte warmly. "Haven't seen you for a while. I expect you've been very busy. Everything all right?"

"I think so," Simon said. "All the plays are in a pretty good place. A lot of final details to see to, but that's what dress rehearsals are for. Just came by to make sure you're ready for *Romeo and Juliet* on Friday."

"We were just talking about that," said Charlotte, "and we are."

"Well, we're not really," said Aaron, "but almost. And we will be."

"Exactly. Someone still has a hat to make."

No one spoke for a moment, and Aaron, sensing an opportunity, cleared his throat. "I think I'll just go find Mattie and see when she's available for her final fitting."

"Fine with me," said Charlotte, turning to Simon for his approval.

"They're all on a break, so this is a good time," agreed Simon. "And while you're there, Aaron, check the props against your list to make sure everything's in place."

When he was gone, Simon turned to Charlotte.

"I've had another update from Brian," he said. "He's doing much better, and he'll definitely be back for the season. Begged me to keep his job open for him. Don't know if he'll be here for dress rehearsal, but at least I don't have to replace him. He was very lucky that this misadventure turned out as well for him as it did."

"Yes, and I'm glad it served as a good wake-up call about the drinking," said Charlotte. "I'm very happy for you that you didn't have to go to all the bother of replacing him." She gave a little laugh. "Although he may think himself irreplaceable. Do you know, I overheard his wife saying something like they'll have trouble finding a place to seat them all? As if Brian could possibly be that much of a draw!"

Simon frowned. "She said that? That doesn't sound like Brian. He's been very humble with me. In his private, reflective, sober moments, he knows his career is in big trouble and that he was very lucky to get this job. He also knows he's struggling to keep it."

That wasn't what Charlotte expected to hear. "Well, maybe he's just been blustering with his wife. Talking himself up to feel better. I don't imagine she does much for his self-esteem." Charlotte thought for a moment. "Or maybe I got it wrong. I was coming out of the kitchen and just caught the tail end of what she was saying, but that's what it sounded like."

Charlotte found it difficult to concentrate on her work after Simon had gone. She puttered about, tidying up the workroom and checking her e-mail for messages and finally gave up and decided to take Rupert for what she called a "thinking walk." He walked and she thought.

Charlotte and Rupert walked often in the wooded area that surrounded the three bungalows. Here, sheltered and well away from the road, it was safe for him to ramble off leash, exploring his favorite haunts, running ahead on his short legs, his corgi bottom wiggling in anticipation, but always turning around to make sure that Charlotte was following. Reassured that she was, he'd then continue on.

She tucked her hands in her pockets and followed Rupert along the same path she and Brian had walked a few weeks earlier. A few yards ahead, something rustling in the dead leaves caught Rupert's attention, and he veered off the path in hot pursuit of a squirrel. The squirrel ran up a tree and glared at Rupert, shaking its tail angrily at him. As he turned to return to Charlotte, he let out a yelp and limped over to her.

"What's happened to you?" she said, bending over. She checked the front paw he had favored. "Oh, no!" The soft pad on his paw had a small nick in it. "Oh, I bet that hurts. Let's get you home and clean it up. But first, let's pick up that glass."

Local teenagers occasionally held field parties in the wooded grounds of the hotel. They could walk here from town and, after a night of drinking, didn't have to worry about someone driving home drunk. In the morning, they'd have left behind the charred remains of a bonfire, empty pizza boxes, squashed beer cans, and sometimes broken liquor bottles. With the snow melted, some of the glass could have been exposed. Charlotte and Rupert weren't far from where Brian had been found, and she supposed he could have been carrying a small bottle that fell out of his coat pocket and shattered.

She left Rupert on the path and walked to the tree where he'd chased the squirrel. She reached into her pocket for a bag to put the pieces of glass in and with her boot stirred the leaves under the tree in broad, sweeping strokes. Her boot caught on something, and when she flicked her foot, the silver handles of a pair of scissors appeared.

She bent over and examined them. She had no doubt they were the missing fabric shears from her workshop.

How did they get here? Who could have taken them? She bent over to pick them up and then withdrew her hand and straightened up. Leaving them where they were, she took off her scarf, tied a knot in one end of it, and threw it up into the branches.

"Come on, Rupert," she said. "Let's get you home. Can you walk?"

He indicated he could, and the two set off. Half an hour later, as Charlotte and Rupert watched from a distance, Ray and Phil, wearing yellow high-visibility jackets, cordoned off the area around the tree with the red scarf fluttering merrily from a lower branch.

"Well?" Charlotte asked Ray as he approached her with the scissors in an evidence bag.

"Well, they're scissors all right," said Ray, holding them up so she could see them. "And you can confirm that these are the scissors from your workshop?"

She fingered them through the bag and nodded.

"No doubt. Yes."

"You'll have to stop in at the station so we can take your fingerprints," Ray said as they walked back to Charlotte's bungalow. "If your prints are on them, we can establish these are the scissors missing from your workshop. And Aaron, too. We'll need his prints as well."

They walked for a few moments in silence, and then Ray said, "The grounds had already been searched, so either they missed the scissors the first time or someone's put them there since."

"You couldn't blame the search team if they did miss them," said Charlotte, "with all the dead leaves everywhere. They were buried under them. And there was snow then, too."

"How is Rupert, by the way?"

"Oh, he's fine. I cleaned his paw and put some cream on it to prevent infection while I waited for you. Thank goodness the cut wasn't deep. Could have been worse, but thanks for asking."

They had arrived at her bungalow and, with Rupert leading the way, climbed the stairs. Ray glanced in the direction of the hotel while she unlocked the door. "Let's sit down," she said when they were all inside. "Coffee?"

"Love one."

When they were settled with their coffees, he leaned toward her. "Tell me," he said. "If I remember correctly, there's a stabbing in *Romeo and Juliet*. How does that work?"

"What do you mean, how does it work?"

"Well, the part with the knife."

Charlotte thought for a moment and then understood what he was asking. "Oh, you mean what kind of knife and where it's kept and all that?" He nodded. "It's a prop knife, not a real one. The actor holds it up so the audience can see it's a knife, then makes a stabbing motion and the blade disappears into the handle. Prop knives are often made out of plastic, and if a real one should be used, someone will make sure the tip has been rounded and the blade blunted so no one can get hurt by acci-dent." Her eyes narrowed slightly. "Why do you ask?"

"Oh, you know me. I like to know all about every-thing. And now tell me about the scissors. Where were they kept?"

"Just on my worktable. There were two pairs. One for fabric only and for paper only. I'm very strict about that."

"So on the worktable. Would anyone have access to them?"

"Yes, I suppose so."

"Did you leave your workroom the morning Lauren was killed?"

"Probably. I can't really remember, but I might have gone to the cafeteria, or the washroom, or any number of places. Or more likely, that morning, I was in and out of the costume storage room, because we were doing the fittings at that time."

"Would you have left the door to your rooms open?"

"I usually do. What are you getting at?"

Ray did not reply, so Charlotte continued.

"But something's occurred to me, and I wonder why I didn't think of this before. When Rupert stepped on the scissors, he yelped. It was quite high pitched, and it was obvious that he was hurt. So why do you suppose when Lauren was stabbed, no one heard anything? Surely she would have cried out, either in pain or surprise? Or maybe even both."

"The assailant grabbed her from behind, and she turned to see who it was just as she was stabbed. One of the scissor blades went in deep and nicked her heart. The killer then lowered her body to the little platform she was standing on, pulled the scissors out, and ran for it."

Charlotte covered her hand with her mouth. Ray continued, "It would have been all over in seconds."

"Do you think it would have taken a lot of strength?" Charlotte asked.

"I don't think so," he replied, "because whoever did it had the element of surprise. It would have been over almost before Lauren knew what was happening. There wasn't a lot of blood, because the blood didn't bleed out of her body but rather filled the sac around the heart, and that's what killed her. It's called a pericardial tamponade, according to the pathologist. The sac fills up and stops the heart from beating. She would have gone into shock very quickly, which is probably why she didn't call out. And if she did, she was at the back of the stage and very weak—just too far away for anyone to hear her."

"Oh, that is so sad. I'm really sorry to hear that."

Ray set his mug on the coffee table and stood up. "Well, I've got to be going. Will I see you later?"

She nodded and checked her watch. "I'm going to Skype with Mum in a few minutes. Call me tonight."

Charlotte looked forward to her Skype visits with her mother at home in Norfolk. Charlotte missed her and worried about her, living on her own. She was just in her late sixties and in relatively good health, but Charlotte knew the time would come when her mother wouldn't be able to cope as well as she used to.

She pressed a few keys on her laptop, and a few seconds later, her mother's smiling face filled the screen.

"Getting on all right, are you, Mum?"

"Oh, yes, darling. Mustn't grumble."

"Tell me all about it."

So for the next fifteen minutes, her mother was off and running. The awful woman who'd moved into number six across the way who drove her children to school in her pajamas and smoked in the car. The price of a good joint! She doubted she'd ever be able to afford to eat beef again. And all the rubbish on television. The women all seemed to be called Cheryl or Katie, and every one of them had ridiculously large breasts. She couldn't tell one Cheryl or Katie from the next. And speaking of television, why can't they make good British drama anymore?

"Well, there's *Downton Abbey*, Mum. You like that."

"Fair enough, I suppose. Oh, I'm sorry, Charlotte, love. All this whinging and moaning. I've been feeling so out of sorts lately. Got a miserable toothache, and you just try getting an appointment with the dentist. You have to suffer for weeks before they can fit you in. Oh, this country's going to hell in a handbasket, let me tell you. You're well out of it. Our best days are behind us. That's all this country's got going for it. Its past."

"I'm sorry to hear about your tooth."

"Well, you just have to make the best of it, don't you? I take a Paracetamol and hope for the best. But honestly, sometimes I can't even concentrate long enough to read my magazine. Anyway, I've been going to the senior drop-in center, and there are some nice people there and they serve a decent cup of tea with a biscuit, so it's good to keep busy."

"What did you just say, Mum?"

"I said it's good to keep busy."

"No, before that. About the toothache."

"Oh, I said I've been taking the Paracetamol tablets and they help with the pain, a little, until I can get in to see the dentist."

"Right. Look, Mum, I'm sorry, but I've got to go. We'll talk soon."

She ended the session and sank back into her sofa. Of course! That's what Lady Deborah had said. Not "seat 'em all." Paracetamol. The British version of Tylenol. She'd just caught the end of the word and had taken it to mean something completely different. *Oh, how could I have been so stupid,* she thought. *If it weren't so awful, it would almost be funny.*

She reached into her handbag and pulled out the business card of the jeweler she had spoken to in New York, the one who had told her the ring was paste. He answered on the third ring.

"Hello," she said. "My name's Charlotte Fairfax, and I was in your store several weeks ago with a ring I asked you to look at. You told me it was fake. Paste. I think you know more about that ring, more than you told me, and I'm hoping you'll be kind enough to answer a couple of questions. Did someone else show you that ring? A young woman, about twenty-three, with dark brown hair?"

Charlotte listened for a moment and then repeated what he'd told her.

"She didn't show it to you, but she took it to a jeweler you know for an appraisal. Right. And she asked a lot of questions about an Englishwoman with a lot of jewelry. And when I came in, because I speak with an English accent, you wondered . . ."

The jeweler spoke for a few more minutes, and then, after thanking him, Charlotte ended the call. She clutched her phone to her chest, thinking furiously. Lady Deborah. A lot of valuable jewelry. Reproductions. And Lauren knew the ring was fake. Did that knowledge get her killed?

She dialed Ray's number. When it went to voice mail, she left a message.

Chapter 28

Aaron was sitting in the workroom, hand-stitching the hat he'd made to accompany his Juliet costume. He held it up for Charlotte to inspect. She took it from him and examined it closely.

"Nice job on the lining," she said. "You can always tell how well made a garment is by checking the seams. It should look as good on the inside as it does on the outside." She handed it back to him. "I'm just going to put the kettle on, make myself a cup of tea, and then we'll have a little chat."

"Am I in trouble?"

"No, of course you're not. Why would you think that?"

"Whenever you say 'a little chat,' I think there's something bad coming. Maybe it's just the way you say it."

For the first time in weeks, Charlotte entered the tiny space not much bigger than a cupboard with a small table, a couple of shelves, a bar refrigerator, and a tiny sink. To call it even a "kitchenette" would have given it higher status than it deserved. A moment later, she called out. "Aaron, *now* you're in trouble! Come here."

He set the hat on the worktable and stood in the doorway of the kitchen cupboard. "What is it?"

Charlotte pointed to the shelf beside the sink. "What's that?"

"It's that can of drink Lauren left on the work table when she was in getting measured. You told me to put in here."

"Yes, I did, but I didn't think I had to tell you to empty it down the sink and then put the can in the recycling. Did you really need to be told to do that? You don't just bring the can in here and leave it here."

"Sorry, Charlotte. My bad." He reached for the can.

"Don't touch it. Unless I'm very much mistaken, the police are going to find it's loaded with Tylenol. Or rather, Paracetamol."

"So you don't want me throw it out?"

"No. I'll let Ray know it's here. In the meantime, neither of us touches it."

"And our 'little chat'?" said Aaron.

"I can't remember now what it was I wanted to speak to you about, but it'll come to me, I'm sure."

"Huh. Well in that case, is it okay if I go back to my hat now? Mattie'll be here any minute for her final fitting, and I want the hat to be ready."

"Right. Off you go, then."

She phoned Ray to tell him about the energy drink can. He told her to expect a visit soon; he wasn't sure who would pick it up, but one of the state police would be along to get it. In the meantime, he reminded her not to touch it. And then she asked a favor of him, which he laughingly agreed was the least he could do.

Charlotte busied herself with a few little tasks, keeping an eye on the door. When Mattie appeared, Aaron rose to greet her. He had covered his dress on the mannequin with a cloth, and Charlotte sensed he was nervous about revealing it to her, although she had reassured him it was beautiful and that Mattie would love it.

Aaron slowly and carefully lifted the muslin cloth from the Juliet costume. When Mattie's face lit up and she reached for it, Charlotte felt the beginnings of a watery glaze fill her eyes. She reached for a tissue and dabbed at them and then joined Aaron and Mattie. Aaron's smile broadened each time Mattie discovered something else she liked about the garment.

"I can't believe you made this just for me!" she exclaimed as she fingered the brocade. "It's absolutely stunning." She turned to Aaron. "How talented you are!"

"All right, Mattie," laughed Charlotte. "That's enough, now. He won't want to return to normal duties if you keep on like that." Aaron laughed good-naturedly but was obviously pleased that his work had found such favor with his client.

"I'll carry it to the screen for you," he told Mattie, "and if you slip it on, we'll do your final fitting." He removed the garment from the stand, carried it to the screen, and disappeared around the back. "It's on the chair," he said, "and here are your ballet slippers," he added, handing them to her. "You'll need to wear them so we can check the length is right."

Charlotte gave Aaron a thumbs-up, and his grin lit up the room.

"I know how lucky I am," came Mattie's disembodied voice from behind the screen. "So many applied for admission to theater school and so few got in. And then, to be chosen to work here this summer and to get a brand-new costume? It doesn't get much better than that." This was followed by a soft rustling sound.

"Do you need any help?" Charlotte asked.

"No, almost ready," she said.

"Aaron, bring down the fan, put it over there on the floor, and switch it on," Charlotte said.

"What?"

"Never mind asking why. Just do it. You'll see when Mattie comes out."

Aaron placed the fan where Charlotte pointed and switched it on. A gentle breeze wafted across the room as Mattie emerged from behind the screen. It caught the bottom of her garment and gave the elegant silk underdress a graceful, billowing lift. Aaron turned to Charlotte with a look of amazement on his face.

"If you want to see how your garment will move," she said, "just use an electric fan. Do you know who taught me that little trick?"

"Who?" said Aaron and Mattie at the same time.

"The Queen's dresser." She turned her gaze toward Mattie. "Now then. Let's see you walk to the door, then turn around and walk back toward us."

When Mattie returned, Charlotte took a couple of steps toward her and then gently put her hands on Mattie's shoulders and pulled them back. "Stand a little straighter, Mattie," she said. "Pretend you're squeezing an orange between your shoulder blades. And take smaller steps. You must walk differently in a long dress than you do in a pair of jeans. Now, off you ago. Try it again. You'll feel the difference."

Mattie repeated her walk to the door, and on the return, a wide grin lit up her face. "I feel taller and more confident," she said.

"I can see you do," said Aaron.

"Right, well, Aaron will finish the fitting now, Mattie. I've got to speak to Simon about something." She picked up her handbag and left the room. Just as she stepped outside the door, she paused to check that she had her glasses.

As she stood there, she heard Aaron respond to something Mattie must have said but that she hadn't heard: "She is. I've learned so much from her. Honestly, I couldn't have done a better internship."

Charlotte took her own advice and stood a little straighter, and with a determined, almost jaunty step, she headed off to find Simon.

She found him backstage, as she expected, sitting at the prompt desk going over his script for the dress rehearsal.

"Simon, glad I caught you. Got a minute?"

"For you, my dear, always."

"Good." She peered out at the empty auditorium. "How about we sit in the front row so we can be comfortable?"

Once they were seated, Charlotte began.

"I've got a favor to ask you. It's about the dress rehearsal this afternoon. I know you expected Aaron to work the prompt desk, but it's very important that he experience the entire production, and I especially want him to see the costume he created for Mattie from front of house. To really get a sense of how costume design works, he needs to see the full production as an audience member."

"That's all very well," said Simon, "but I need a prompter if we're to have a full production. I need to see the play from front of house, too. I can't do it."

"I thought of that, so I found a volunteer to work the prompt desk."

When she told him who, he raised an amused eyebrow. "Really?"

*

Charlotte's workroom was empty. "Gone for a coffee with Mattie," read the little note on the scratch piece of paper on her desk. She smiled and reached for her handbag. Just as she opened it, a soft knock on the door made her turn around. It was Brian. He was wearing some of his costume and was in full stage makeup. The heavily drawn dark lines on his face made him look grotesque up close.

"Could I have a word?" he said.

"Yes, of course. Come in." She pointed at a chair near her desk and they sat, awkwardly but not uncomfortably. He looked different. Thinner in the face.

"You're looking much better than the last time I saw you," said Charlotte.

"Yes, I feel much better," he said. He lowered his eyes and fiddled with the large costume ring on his finger. "I made a huge mess of everything," he said. "I wanted to apologize to you."

"You don't need to apologize to me."

"Oh, yes, I do. Look, the play's starting soon, and this isn't the right time, but later, I was hoping we could talk. I want to explain—"

"Brian, it's okay."

"No, it's not okay. It's unfinished business. Can we talk?"

"If you like. But for now, you need to finish getting dressed. You don't want to be late."

"No." He stood up.

"You look as if you've lost a little weight," she commented. "Are your costumes fitting okay? If not, we can adjust them."

"They're fine for now, but thanks for asking."

She sat quietly for a moment after he'd gone. The only thing she'd smelled on him was the distinctive, unforgettable smell of stage makeup, like a sweet, heavy crayon.

*

"Right, now, everybody, gather round, please." The cast members, in full costume and stage makeup, crowded together backstage, smiling nervously and encouragingly at one another.

"This is it," Simon said. "Well, almost. Dress rehearsals. Previews. This is when all our hard work starts to pay off. Everything you've all been working so hard for is about to come to life. We've got some local high school students and many of their parents in this afternoon, and they're expecting your best. So let's go, everybody. Break a leg!" The cast members clapped and took their places, ready for curtain up.

"Oh, good, here you are," Simon said to Ray. "Almost didn't recognize you out of uniform." He handed Ray a prompt book and said, "Follow me." He led him to the prompter's table with its little desk lamp, just out of sight of the audience. "Just follow along as the actors speak their lines, and if someone hesitates or seems lost, he'll look to you for help. Just give him his next line in a loud whisper."

"Got that." Ray smiled. "This should be fun."

The last of the audience took their seats, and as the lights dimmed, the casual chatting stopped and an expectant hush fell over the audience. In the quiet semi-darkness, the tragedy of two households of Verona, both alike in dignity, began to unfold. It didn't take long for Charlotte to be drawn deeper into the world of the two star-crossed lovers, and as the time approached for Brian to make his entrance, she found herself growing nervous for him.

And then, with a dramatic flourish of a fur-trimmed, midnight-blue cloak befitting a nobleman, there he was. He paused as he arrived onstage, giving the audience a sly look, as if inviting them to applaud. *And long ago, and in a different place,* thought Charlotte, *they would have.* When they couldn't get enough of Brian and his majestic voice. But now, no one really knew who he was.

Suddenly, the years fell away, and she was in her early twenties, standing in the wings of the main stage at Stratford-upon-Avon, watching Brian own the stage as Hamlet. His deep tenor voice resonated with pain, and everyone in the audience felt his mounting anguish. As he stepped off stage, he caught her by the waist and briefly pulled her to him before racing to his dressing room for a quick break. And a quick drink. It fueled his performance, he said. Kept him at the top of the game. Until it began to let him down. And then it was his turn to let her down.

She stole a glance at Aaron on her right. He was entranced with the production, swept away on a tide of emotion.

And then the nurse called out, "Anon, anon! Come, let's away; the strangers all are gone," signaling the end of act 1. The drama continued to unfold, drawing everyone deeper into the coming tragedy, until it was time for intermission.

As the house lights came back up, Charlotte turned to Aaron.

"Go backstage quickly and make sure everyone's costumes are all right. Sometimes things snap or come undone and they need a quick repair during the intermission. And be sure to tell them they're doing great and everybody's loving it. Give them some encouragement." Aaron left his seat, ran up the stage steps, and disappeared behind the curtain. Charlotte twisted in her seat and scanned the audience behind her.

There was no sign of Lady Deborah. Perhaps she thought that Brian no longer deserved her support. Or it might be that she'd seen him perform so many times that it was all wasted on her now. Or maybe she just had better things to do.

Star-crossed lovers, thought Charlotte. Was that what Brian and Lauren had been? She doubted it; they'd only known each other two or three weeks. That hardly seemed long enough for him to give her a ring, but then drunkards often did daft things they later regretted.

She spent the rest of the play thinking about the ring, the jewelry . . . she was sure that the key to all this lay in the jewelry. And then she realized she needed to spend a little time on the Internet. There were bloggers who paid close attention to the jewelry collections of royalty and nobility. Who wore what to every event. And these bloggers were often knowledgeable about the history and provenance of the jewels. And she needed to know more about Lady Deborah's father, Lord Roxborough. He must be . . . what? In his mid-eighties?

The play ended to enthusiastic clapping, and as the cast took their curtain calls, Brian especially seemed to cherish the applause, drinking it in greedily and lingering just a moment too long. Charlotte thought Mattie looked lovely in the costume Aaron had designed and made for her, and she told him so, in a soft whisper.

As the audience stood up and prepared to leave, the curtains swished back, and Ray came down the side stairs to join her.

"Did you enjoy it?" Charlotte asked.

"I did. Only had to give two prompts. One to Mrs. Capulet, who I noticed was not wearing any nice rings."

Charlotte winced. "We do have a few pieces of jewelry in our store room, of course," she said a little stiffly, "but nothing that would have been appropriate for her."

He grinned at her.

"So," she said, "before I forget—final dress rehearsal tomorrow and then a few of us are meeting up in my wardrobe room to toast the new season. Would you like to join us?"

"I'd love to. Simon's asked me to do the prompts again. I'm starting to think of that chair as the best seat in the house."

He looked out at the auditorium and then back to Charlotte in front of him.

"Well, come on," Ray said. "Let's wrap everything up here, and then I'd like to take you to dinner."

"Oh, I would love that. It's exactly what I need. And will there be wine with this dinner?"

*

Toward morning, as the first glimmer of muted light filtered through the blinds, turning Charlotte's bedroom from black to a pale grey, Ray eased himself quietly out of bed. She stirred and looked up at him, her hair tousled and her eyes brimming with sleep.

"Sorry," he said softly. "Didn't want to wake you. I'm on early shift this morning so I can get away in time for the rehearsal this afternoon. I'll call you later." He bent over, kissed her, and then disappeared into the bathroom. The sound of running water was soon followed by a door being closed quietly. She sighed and got out of bed and then padded through the living room and kitchen to lock the door behind him. *I'm not a policeman's girlfriend for nothing*, she thought.

She glanced at Rupert, curled up in his basket, and filled the kettle. While she waited for it to boil, she returned to her bedroom to get a warm dressing gown and slippers. She made herself a cup of coffee and then took it with her to the bedroom to get dressed.

As she pulled a sweater over her head, she thought about something Ray had said at dinner last night. Although they'd agreed not to discuss the case, of course they had, and something had slipped into the conversation that now troubled her. Brian and Lady Deborah could offer each other alibis, he'd said. But that wasn't quite right.

Aaron had seen Lady Deborah at the time Lauren was killed, but he hadn't thought anything of it because he saw her all the time, lifting bags in and out of her car, setting off for the train station, or coming home just before dark. People don't pay attention to things that are familiar; they notice things that are not familiar.

Everybody, including the police, kept asking him if he saw anyone who wasn't supposed to be there. As far as Aaron was concerned, it was only Lady What's-her-name, doing what she always did.

A chill ran through Charlotte. She was convinced that Aaron hadn't seen Lady Deborah getting ready to go into the city as usual; he'd seen her hiding the murder weapon in the trunk of her car. And if she wasn't very much mistaken, the DNA evidence would be in a Saks or Barneys bag.

Chapter 29

She called Ray to tell him what she suspected, and then much to Rupert's delight at such an early outing, the two set off on their morning walk. Just as they reached the path that led to the parkland adjacent to the hotel, the door to the Prentice bungalow opened, and Lady Deborah, wearing her camel-colored coat, picked her way down the three steps, using two hands to carry a black suitcase. She set the case down beside the car while she opened the trunk and then lifted the case, rested it for a moment on the bumper, and then tipped it over the side. It disappeared into the trunk, and she slammed the lid shut.

She took a step back, turned, and found Charlotte, with Rupert on his leash, standing beside her.

"Oh! You startled me, creeping up on me like that! What are you doing here? I'm in a bit of a hurry. What do you want?"

"Hello, Deborah." Charlotte tipped her head in the direction of the trunk. "Going somewhere nice?"

"I don't see how that's any of your business." Deborah's eyes blazed as she took a step toward Charlotte. "Now I really must ask you to step out of my way. I need to get going."

"Are you sure you've got everything?"

Deborah shot her a look of high haughtiness infused with a vague uncertainty. "Yes, I think so. What's it to you?"

"Your Saks and Barneys bags? In the trunk, are they?"

Deborah hesitated, as if thinking over very carefully what she wanted to say. "You know, this is starting to get tiresome. I really can't be bothered with this conversation anymore, or you either, for that matter. Now, for the last time, please get out of my way and let me get in my car, or I'll—"

"You'll what, Deborah? Kill me, like you killed Lauren because she got in your way? Because she'd discovered the ring that Brian gave her was fake and she worked out that you were getting copies made of your jewelry?

"I don't think she quite understood the implications, but you couldn't take that chance, could you? So you tried to kill her with an overdose of acetaminophen, which you had on hand because you get frequent headaches. In the U.K., it's called Paracetamol. Here in the U.S., it's Tylenol. But it's the same thing. That's what you were saying to Ray at the bungalow that morning when

Brian had been hurt. Paracetamol. And I just heard the tail end and thought you'd said, 'seat 'em all!'"

Charlotte was desperate to check the time on her phone. How long had they been talking? Where was Ray? If Deborah got away now, they might never find her. She had to keep stalling. Keep the conversation, one-sided as it was, going.

"It wouldn't have been hard for you to crush up Paracetamol tablets and slip them into Lauren's energy drink," she continued. "After all, she carried cans of it around with her the way most people carry coffee, and she set down opened cans all over the place. And a fairly small Tylenol overdose can do a lot of damage, especially to the liver."

"Surely I can get copies made of my own jewelry if I want to," Lady Deborah replied. "So your little theory is just that. A stupid little theory."

"Ah, but it's not your jewelry, though, is it?" said Charlotte. "It's tied up with the laws of British primogeniture. The jewels belong to your father, just like the manor house, the title, and the artwork, and they'll go to your brother when he inherits.

"Or they would have done, but I expect the pieces have been broken up by now for the individual gemstones. You've sold them, haven't you? Sold the originals, and used the copies to cover it up."

Lady Deborah sniffed, looking down her nose. "This is nonsense, all of it. Now get out of my way, before I—"

"The only one you couldn't bear to part with was your mother's engagement ring," Charlotte said, "so that's why you still have the original that you wore to the welcome party and the copy that Brian gave to Lauren.

"And that's why you had to kill Lauren when she recovered from the Paracetamol overdose you gave her. She knew what you were doing with the jewels, and she would have worked out pretty quickly who had it in for her. Maybe she already had. So you took my scissors, went looking for her, and seized the opportunity to kill her."

"They're your scissors," Deborah snarled. "Maybe you killed her. Now for the last time, get the hell out of my way. I'm not going to stand here and listen to any more of this rubbish."

When Charlotte didn't move, she took a step toward her.

"I mean it. Move." The menace in her tone was unmistakable.

"Or what?"

"Or I'll kill him." She pointed at Rupert, who looked up at her with a cheeky smile. "I swear to God, I will. I'll run him over, and who's to say it wasn't an accident?"

Charlotte hesitated, and then sensing Deborah's desperation and frightened by the hard look of hatred in her eyes, she stepped to one side, making sure Rupert was safely beside her. Lady Deborah got in the car and started it. She backed up a few feet, stopped, rolled down the window, and threw something out. She then put the car in drive and sped off. Charlotte picked up the key on the Statue of Liberty keychain that she'd thrown out the window and slowly wrapped her fingers around it.

"Well, we did the best we could, Rupert," she said. "There she goes."

Lady Deborah's car slowed as it approached the end of the driveway that led from the hotel property to the main road. At that moment, two police cars with flashing lights turned into the driveway, boxing her in.

Relieved that the police had arrived in time, Charlotte smiled as she imagined Deborah, all airs and graces, demanding to know the meaning of this. She laughed when she thought how this would go down with Ray, as he politely asked her to open the trunk.

Chapter 30

Late Saturday afternoon, after the final dress rehearsal, Aaron, his uncle Harvey, and Simon joined Ray and Charlotte in the costume department for a glass of champagne to celebrate the opening of the new season. Dress rehearsals were wrapped, and previews started next week, with opening night next weekend. The hotel was filling up, and media tickets for opening night were being snapped up. Harvey had been right. The season promised to be the best one in a very long time, and this really could be the year that Jacobs Grand Hotel and the Catskills Shakespeare Theater Company turned the corner.

"There's something I want to discuss with you," Charlotte had said to Ray over dinner the night before. "It's to do with me. Well, me and Simon."

Ray's stomach had clenched as his heart thudded against his rib cage.

"I've been thinking about this for a while, and now seems like the right time," she had begun. "Mattie Lane—the young actress who plays Juliet—was saying how difficult it was to get into theater school . . . there's much more demand than places available. So I thought that, with Simon's New York connections, we could start a theater school, here, at the hotel. I can teach costume and set design, and he can teach the acting and directing, that side of it. The hotel will provide the residence facility. We'll do it on a regular semester system, September to April. And of course, the students become the actors for the summer season. Oh, there are millions of details to work out, but I think the idea in general is a good one.

"I haven't said anything to Simon yet because I wanted to see what you think. It would bring lots of students into the area, the cafes and bars will do more business, and the hotel will be viable."

He had looked at her across the table from him, her eyes shining, lips slightly parted, fresh and beautiful, and in that moment, realized he'd fallen in love with her. And compared to what he had thought she was going to tell him, a theater-school proposal was good news.

He had reached out, taken her hand, and given her a wide, open smile.

"I think it's a terrific idea, and I know you'll make a huge success of it."

"Great! I'll talk to Simon in the morning. It'll be a tremendous challenge, but I think we can make it work." She had laughed. "Make it work!"

She had tilted her head and smiled at him. "And you do know there's nothing going on between Simon and me, I hope? It would simply be a business arrangement. We're colleagues. Nothing more."

His heart had calmed down, and he had taken a sip of wine. It had never tasted better.

Now, sitting in the costume department with her friends, Charlotte could sense a feeling of excitement built on an underlying layer of creative confidence she had not experienced in the previous ten seasons.

"I asked Brian to join us," Simon told the little gathering. "He's just getting changed and taking off his makeup, and he'll be along soon. With his wife arrested this morning, asking him to join us seemed the least we could do. He knows there'll be champagne, and he's fine with that. He's been going to AA, and so far, so good."

A few minutes later, Brian stood uncertainly in the doorway.

Charlotte smiled at him. "Brian! Come in."

"You did a terrific job on stage today, Brian," Simon said, and the little group broke into applause. "You gave a wonderful performance under difficult circumstances. Well done. I was really proud of you."

"Actually, it took my mind off things," Brian said. "Isn't that the purpose of theater? To provide an escape from our ordinary lives for two or three hours? Well, it does that for the performers, too."

Charlotte handed him a glass of mineral water with a slice of lemon, and he moved easily through the group, talking to everyone. Half an hour later, one by one, starting with Phil, they set down their glasses, thanked Charlotte, and departed, until only she, Brian, and Aaron remained.

"I'm meeting Mattie now for a coffee," Aaron said, "but I'll be back to help you tidy up."

Left alone with Brian, she gestured to the chair beside her desk.

"I just wanted you to know," he said, "that marrying her was the biggest mistake of my life. I barely even knew her, just met her at a party, and then she asked me to marry her."

"She asked you?" Charlotte said.

"Yes, and I admit I was weak. I thought I was going places, and I fell for the title, the landed gentry family with the big house—all that. I thought marrying her would enhance my reputation. It just brought me a load of misery. I knew within weeks marrying her had been a big mistake."

"Then why did you stay with her?" Charlotte asked. "You didn't have to, in this day and age."

"I've asked myself that a lot, lately," Brian said. "Laziness, habit, certainly—but mostly money."

"Money? You mean her money?"

He nodded. "Her family is old-school Catholic, you see. Her father never approved of our marriage and warned her he'd cut her off without a penny if we divorced. So we mostly lived separate lives on the understanding there could be no divorce. But her father's got dementia now, and barely knows who we are. So we'd been discussing it. Honestly, I don't think she cared one way or the other. And frankly, neither did I."

He drained the last of his mineral water and stood up.

"Even if all this hadn't happened, we couldn't have gone on much longer. We just didn't care."

He looked around for a place to set the glass, and Charlotte held out her hand to take it.

"I know it's too late for us," he said. "You've got a new life here. But I hope we can be friends."

"I don't know about friends, but we can certainly be professional. Colleagues on friendly terms, perhaps."

He hesitated for a moment, as if unsure if any kind of parting gesture, such as a hug, would be appropriate. Deciding against it, much to her relief, he gave her a brief smile and left.

She was still standing there holding the glass when Aaron returned. He picked up the empty champagne bottles and took them to the tiny kitchenette off the workroom. As they clattered into the recycling bin, she set Brian's tumbler on the tray beside the champagne flutes for Aaron to return to the canteen.

"Did you know that champagne is the only beverage you should allow in an actor's dressing room?" she asked him when he returned to the workroom, wiping his hands on a paper towel.

"No," he said. "Why's that?"

"Because if you spill a few drops, it's the only drink that won't stain your fabric."

And this time, Aaron beat her to it. "Who taught you that?"

"Coco Chanel."

"Finally! Someone I've heard of!"

Acknowledgments

I'm enormously grateful to Matthew Martz for the opportunity to be among the first authors published by Crooked Lane Books. My thanks to his colleague, Nike Power, for her sharp editing of the manuscript and excellent suggestions for improvement.

Charlotte Dean, who has designed costumes and sets for theaters across Canada, including the Stratford Festival, the Shaw Festival, and the Royal Manitoba Theatre Centre, kindly provided insight into the fascinating process of creating the costumes that bring a theater production to life. Her expertise on how it all works was invaluable—any errors are mine.

Thank you to Hannah Dennison and Sylvia Jones for taking the time to read the manuscript and as always, special thanks to my literary agent Dominick Abel for his wise counsel and never-ending support.

Don't miss
Elizabeth J. Duncan's

Ill Met by Murder

Available December 13, 2016
from Crooked Lane Books

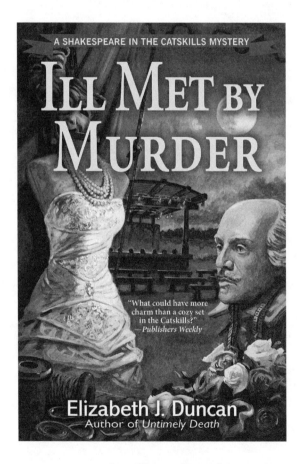